PHINEAS

He was free, fearless, the envy of everyone—and completely unsuspecting of the one who betrayed him.

CHRISTOPHER

With his father dead and his mother sole heir to the fortune, there was only Ernie—and he had to travel 5,000 miles to find out that Ernie didn't want him either.

LAWRENCE

He was neither grotesque nor courageous enough to make a mark—but for one single act he would always be remembered.

Books by John Knowles
Ask your bookseller for the books you have missed

A SEPARATE PEACE
MORNING IN ANTIBES
DOUBLE VISION:
AMERICAN THOUGHTS ABROAD
INDIAN SUMMER
PHINEAS

Published by Bantam Books, Inc.

Phineas

John Knowles

Six Stories

BANTAM BOOKS · TORONTO · NEW YORK · LONDON

A NATIONAL GENERAL COMPANY

*This low-priced Bantam Book
has been completely reset in a type face
designed for easy reading, and was printed
from new plates. It contains the complete
text of the original hard-cover edition.*
NOT ONE WORD HAS BEEN OMITTED.

RLI: VLM 9.0
IL 8.12

PHINEAS: SIX STORIES

*A Bantam Book / published by arrangement with
Random House, Inc.*

*PRINTING HISTORY
Random House edition published October 1968
Bantam edition published December 1969
2nd printing
3rd printing*

*Bantam Books are published by Bantam Books, Inc., a National
General company. Its trade-mark, consisting of the words "Bantam
Books" and the portrayal of a bantam, is registered in the United
States Patent Office and in other countries. Marca Registrada.
Bantam Books, Inc., 666 Fifth Avenue, New York, N.Y. 10019.*

PRINTED IN THE UNITED STATES OF AMERICA

To
Corrin Peter Strong

Contents

1	A Turn with the Sun	1
2	Summer Street	29
3	The Peeping Tom	55
4	Martin the Fisherman	85
5	Phineas	97
6	The Reading of the Will	119

Phineas

A
Turn
with the Sun

It was dusk; the warm air of the early spring afternoon was edged with an exhilarating chill, and in the half-light the dark green turf of the playing field acquired the smooth perfection of a thick rug, spreading up to the thin woods, lightly brushed with color along one sideline, and down to the river, with the stolid little bridge arching over it, along the other. Across the stream more playing fields, appearing smoother still in the distance, sloped gently up to the square gray shape of the gymnasium; and behind it the towers and turrets of the boys' school were etched against the darkening blue sky.

The game was over, and the Red team, pleased by their three-to-two victory, but only mildly pleased since it was just an intramural game, formed a loose circle and cheered for themselves and their opponents: "Reds, Reds, Reds, Reds, rah, rah, rah, Blues!" A few players tarried for some extra shots at the cage, which the second-string Blue goalie made half-hearted attempts to defend; but most of them straggled on toward the bridge, swinging their lacrosse sticks carelessly along beside them. Three boys played catch as they went; one of them missed a pass near the bridge and the ball plopped into the stream. "Nuts," he said, "I'm not going in after it." "No, too cold," the others agreed.

As Lawrence Stewart stepped onto the gravel road leading over the bridge, he experienced that thrill of feeling himself strong and athletic which the sound of his cleats on a hard surface always excited. His stride altered perceptibly, became more free-swinging, authoritative. "I scored," he said simply, "d'you see that, Bead? I scored my first goal."

"Yeah," Bead's scratchy voice had an overtone of cordiality, "good going, boy. The winning point too."

They crunched along in silence up to the bridge, and then Lawrence was emboldened to issue an invitation. "You going to the flick tonight? I mean I guess it's Shelley Winters or someone . . . "

Bead balanced his companion's possible new status for an indecisive instant, and then elected to hedge. "Yeah, well, I'll see you after dinner in the Butt Room for a smoke. I'm prob'ly going. Bruce," he added with careful casualness, "said something about it."

Bruce! Lawrence sensed once again that he was helplessly sliding back, slowly but inexorably, into the foggy social bottomland where unacceptable first-year boys dwell. He had risen out of it just now: the goal he had scored, the sweaty ease of his body, the *grump-grump* of his shoes on the gravel had suggested something better for him. But here was Bead, like himself, only seven months at the school, and yet going to the movies with Bruce. Lawrence marveled at the speed with which Bead was settling into the school, and he marveled again at his own failure, after seven months, to win a single close friend.

4

Not that Lawrence was a pariah; the hockey captain had never invaded his room, as he had Fruitcake Putsby's next door, and festooned his clothes through the hall, he had never found a mixture of sour cream and Rice Krispies in his bed at night, no one had ever poured ink into the tub while he was bathing. The victims of such violations were genuine outcasts, but the very fact of their persecutions had, Lawrence reflected, some kind of negative value. They were at least notable in their way. ("There goes Fruitcake Putsby!" someone would shout. "Hi ya, Fruitie"). They had a status all their own; and a few of them, by senior year, could succeed by some miraculous alchemy in becoming accepted and even respected by the whole school for what they were and could not help but be, like the monstrous old city hall which the townspeople come to love because it is crazy and theirs.

Lawrence was neither grotesque enough nor courageous enough for that. He merely inhabited the nether world of the unregarded, where no one bothered him or bothered about him. Why, after all, should they? He had entered in fourth-form year, when the class was already clearly stratified, he arrived knowing only one person in the school, he came from a small Virginia town which no one had ever heard of, he was unremarkable athletically, his clothes were wrong, his vocabulary was wrong, and when he talked at all it was about the wrong things.

He had been assigned to an out-of-the-way house (instead of to one of the exuberant dormitories) with six other nebulous flotsam, and there on the edge of the school he had been waiting all year for something to happen to him, living alone in a little room tucked up under the eaves.

His failure to strike out in some, in any, direction

5

puzzled him in October, when he had been at Devon six weeks, angered him in December, made him contemptuous in February, and on this burgeoning April day when everything else stirred with life, took on the coloration of tragedy. He crossed over the bridge with Bead, and his heart stopped for an instant as it always did on this bridge; in his imagination he again stood on the railing, with his image white and mysterious in the green-black water twenty-five feet below, and he leaped out and over, as he had done last September on his fourth day there, somersaulting twice while most of the school looked on in admiration at the new boy, and knifed cleanly into the icy water.

Last September, his fourth day at school. He hadn't been thinking of anything in particular there on the bridge; everyone was diving from it, so he did too. When he plunged from the railing he had been just another of the unknown new boys, but when he broke the surface of the water in that remarkable dive, one that he had never attempted before and was never to repeat, he became for his schoolmates a boy to be considered. That is why Ging Powers, a senior from his own town who had seemed these first days to be decisively avoiding him, came over in the shower room afterward and dropped an invitation to dinner like a negligible piece of soap. "Come over to the Inn for dinner tonight. Got a couple of friends I want you to meet."

There is a trophy room in the Devon School gymnasium much visited by returning alumni; during June reunions they wander whispering past its softly lighted cases, in which gleam the cups and medals of athletic greatness. Proud banners hang from its paneled walls, inscribed with the records of triumphant, forgotten afternoons. It is like a small, peculiarly sacred chapel in a great cathedral, in which the echoes of hymns can be heard by those who would listen. At the far end, standing long and bright in the focal niche, the alumni would admire the James Harvey Fullerton Cup, Awarded Each Year to That Member of the Sixth Form Who, in the Opinion of his Fellows and Masters, Most Closely Exemplifies the Highest Traditions of Devon. There is no mention of athletics in the inscription, but the cup has come to rest in the gymnasium, in the place of honor, because the highest tradition of Devon is the thinking athlete. Thirty-four names have been engraved on its burnished surface since Mr. Fullerton, feeling disturbed by the activities of German submarines, decided to confirm the reality of his untroubled childhood by donating it, with a small endowment, to his old school. The submarines are now gone, along with Mr. Fullerton, even the Fullerton Mills have passed into other hands; but the cup, born of anxiety, lives serenely on, gleaming like some symbol of royalty in the Devon School trophy room.

Lawrence approached it that afternoon, his fourth at the school, and was struck by the beauty and sacredness of the place. This surely was the heart of Devon: the chapel was like an assembly hall, the library was a clearing house, the houses were dormitories, the classrooms, classrooms; only here did he sense that behind the visible were deeper meanings, that everything stood for something else, that these trophies and banners were clues to the hidden core of the school. He left the gymnasium lost in thought.

He had felt he was still in the air as he walked from the gym back to his room that afternoon, still spinning down upon his own bright image in the murky water. He dressed hurriedly for the dinner at the Inn, for this was surely the beginning of his career at Devon. He explained how wonderfully everything was going in an ardent letter to Janine which he had just time to dash off, and then walked, holding himself back from running by an intoxicating exercise of will power, and arrived at last at the Inn. Everything within him was released; it was as though his dive into the river had washed away his boyhood, and he now stood, clean and happy, wondering dreamily what he would be like now.

The hushed dining room was pervaded by the atmosphere of middle-aged gentility characteristic of Inns at boys' schools: the dull walnut woodwork, the pink-and-green wallpaper depicting Colonial scenes, the virginal fireplace. At the far end of the room Lawrence saw his dinner partners huddled conspiratorily at a corner table. He wheeled past other, empty tables, bright with white cloths and silver, realized dimly that there were murmuring groups dining here and there in the room; and then Ging, his thin, segmented frame unfolding from a chair, was muttering introductions. "This is Vinnie Ump," he seemed to say, and Lawrence recognized Vinnie James, vice-chairman of the senior council, a calm, blond Bostonian who was allowed to be as articulate as he chose because he was so unassertively sure of himself. "And this," said Ging, in a somewhat more stately cadence, "is Charles Morrell." Lawrence recognized him too, of course; this was Morrell, the fabled "Captain Marvel" of the football field, the baseball field, and the hocky rink. Lawrence had never seen him at close quarters before; he seemed more formidable than ever.

Vinnie James was talking, and after pausing for a neutral, birdlike nod to Lawrence, he continued, "So if you want to put up with being patronized by a lot of crashing bores, then you can go to Harvard, and be Punched all sophomore year."

Captain Marvel leaned his heavily handsome face out over the table. "I don't get you, Vinnie, what's this 'Punching'?"

"That's how you get into the clubs at Harvard, Dim One." Vinnie's eyes flickered humorously at him for an instant. "They invite you to Punch parties all sophomore year, and when they stop inviting you, then you know you're not going to be asked to join the club."

"Well," Ging looked with masked apprehension from one to the other, "they've got to take *some* guys, don't they? And Devon isn't such a bad background."

"It's not Groton," said Vinnie mercilessly, "of course."

"Groton!" Ging clutched his tastefully striped tie savagely. "I wouldn't be caught dead at that snobatorium. I could've, if I'd wanted to I could've gone to Groton. But Mother said wild horses couldn't drag a son of hers to that snobatorium. Not anybody of hers, to *that* place!"

Lawrence felt dizzy at the barefacedness of this lie. He knew that Mrs. Powers would cheerfully have violated most of the customs of civilization to get a son of hers into Groton. Devon had been a hasty compromise after Groton had proved out of the question.

"In any case," Vinnie remarked dryly, "Marvel here won't have any trouble. Personable athletes are kidnapped by the most desirable clubs the moment they appear." Both Ging and Captain Marvel were headed for Harvard, but Vinnie made no comment on Ging's chances.

Lawrence disliked and felt superior to Ging at once. The climber! What a lying climber. He had never realized before what a fool Ging was; it made him feel older to realize it now. It was so clear when you could see him beside Captain Marvel, cool, unconcerned Marvel, who would easily rise to the top of every group he entered, leaving Ging clawing and snarling below. Ging's very face seemed to alter before Lawrence's wide eyes; where he had seen authority he now saw pretentiousness, eyes that appeared alert were now apprehensive, the long, prominent nose, patrician before, was now ludicrous, woeful.

Lawrence looked away irritably, regretting that it was Ging who had introduced him to the others. At the same time he felt himself more thoroughly aware than he had ever been of how the world went, of who fitted where, of what was grand and genuine and what was shoddy and fake. Devon had posed a question to him, had demanded that he do something. This afternoon he had done a single, beautiful dive; it was just right and he knew it the moment he hit the water. And now he had come to understand Captain Marvel. The answer was athletics; not just winning a major D, not health or muscles or some other byproduct, but the personality of the athlete itself, the unconscious authority which his strength, his skill, his acclaim gave him. Lawrence stirred his tomato soup reflectively and felt his diffuse ambitions coming into focus, experienced a vision of himself as the Majestic Athlete; he decided instinctively and immediately to accept it, there at dinner among the walnut and silver and the polite murmurings of the other diners. He gathered about himself the mantle of the Olympiad, and lost in its folds, he burst into speech.

"I have some cousins, two cousins, you know, Ging—George and Carter—they're in clubs at Harvard, I mean a club at Harvard, one club, both of 'em are in the same club. It's the ... the ... " Lawrence was suddenly stricken with the thought that George and Carter might very easily not be in the best Harvard club, or even the second best; but everyone, even Marvel, was listening with interest. "It's called," he felt his color rising at the inelegance of the name, "the Gas—or something."

"Oh, yes," said Vinnie crisply, "that's a very good club, for New Yorkers mostly, they have some very good men."

"Oh," Lawrence breathed with fake innocence and real relief. This success swept him spinning on. "George and Carter, they go there for dinners, but they always have lunch in the—is it the Houses?" his wide, brightened blue eyes searched his listeners' faces avidly; Vinnie nodded a brief assent. "They said those clubs make you so ingrown, you just know all these fancy socialites and everything and they wanted to know, you know, everybody; they didn't want to be exclusive or anything like that. It isn't like up here, I mean there isn't—aren't all these clubs and things. They said that I'd get raided and my bed pied and all, but nothing like that seems to happen up here; but they did say that when I went on to Harvard, if I do go there, that after being here it'll be easier and I'll know people and not have to study, but I don't really study so hard here, 'course it's only been four days, but after what everybody said about prep school I thought I'd be studying all the time, but, well, take this afternoon"—that was good, *take this afternoon* smacked of maturity; he paused an instant for the two important seniors (Ging was a bystander now) to catch the overtone of authority in it—"we went swimming off the bridge, and that flip, I thought a two-and-a-half flip might be tough, but ... " he paused again, hoping Ging might make himself useful as a witness to this feat; nothing happened, so he finished a little out of breath, "it wasn't."

"Yeah," Captain Marvel said, "I saw you do it."

This swept down Lawrence's last controls. His best moment had been seen, and doubtless admired, by the most important athlete in school. He rushed ahead now, eager to impress him even more; no, by golly, he was through impressing people. Now he was ready to leap, in one magnificent bound, to the very peak of his ambitions, to become Captain Marvel's protégé, to learn what it meant to be unconcerned, powerful, and a man. So he stuttered gaily on, snatching at everything inside him that seemed presentable—home, his family, Janine, the play he had seen in New York; he assumed every grown-up attitude he could find. All of it he brought forth, as an offering of fealty.

The seniors followed this unwinding of a new boy carefully, looked where he pointed, gauging all his information and attitudes according to their own more precisely graded yardsticks, and took his measure. What they did not think to measure, because it didn't seem important, was his vitality.

"Devon is like some kind of country club-penitentiary, where the inmates don't take walks around the courtyard, they go to the private penitentiary golf course for eighteen holes. And the dean, is that who he is? that queer, stuttery old bird, you know, the one in chapel the first day, the one who looks like Hoover with an Oxford accent ... "

"Yes, that's the dean," said Vinnie, fingering his water glass, "Dean Eleazer Markham Bings-Smith."

"No," exploded Lawrence, "is that his name? His honest name?" He regretted the *honest,* it should have been *actual.*

"Why does he talk that way, and look that way? Like my beagle, that's the way he looks, like the beagle I've got at home, my beagle looks just like that right after he's had a bath."

There was something like consternation passing around the table. Lawrence felt it and looked wonderingly from one to the other. Ging was watching an elderly couple making their way toward the door. The others examined their desserts.

"Was that the dean?" Lawrence asked in a shocked whisper. "Did he hear me?"

No one really answered, but Lawrence, alive in every nerve now, responded symbolically. He slipped like a boneless organism from his chair and sank beneath the table; there he performed the appropriate expiation; he banged his head, not too hard, against the table's underside.

There was a scraping of chairs. Lawrence saw napkins flutter onto the seats, and suddenly he realized the impossibility of his position: under a table in the Anthony Wayne Dining Room of the Devon Inn, making a fool of himself.

He could not recall afterward how he got to his feet, but he remembered very clearly what was said.

"I have an appointment," Vinnie was informing Ging, and then to Lawrence, "That was not the dean, that was Dr. Farnham, the registrar. I doubt whether he heard you. And if he did, I doubt whether he knows or cares *who* you are."

"Are you British?" demanded Captain Marvel with heavy distaste. "Is that why you talk so queer?"

Lawrence felt the exuberance within him turn over then, leaving a sob pressing against his chest.

13

He could not speak and would not cry, but drew a deep, shuddering breath.

Marvel and Vinnie strode purposefully out through the door, Ging followed, and Lawrence roamed out a few paces behind, out into the damp September night, down the deserted street to the quadrangel where the dormitory lights streamed hospitably from cozy windows. Ging said "G'night" there as though he were saying "Pass" during a dull bridge game, and Lawrence was left to wander down the lane to the cluttered old house, to the little room stuck up under the eaves where he lived.

In the next weeks, after the first storms had subsided, Lawrence tried again and again to analyze his failure. Whom had he offended, how, why? Why was everything he had ever wanted sparkling like a trophy in his hands one minute and smashed to bits at his feet the next?

Defeat seemed to follow upon defeat after that. Having missed the peak of his ambition, he assumed that lesser heights could be attained automatically; he felt like a veteran of violent foreign wars whose scars entitled him to homage and precedence. Instead he was battered on every occasion: one day he offered to move into the empty half of a double room down the hall and the boy living there had simply ignored him, had pretended not to hear. Then he turned wildly delinquent; he threw his small steamer trunk, filled with shoes and books, down the long flight of stairs under which the housemaster lived. It slammed against Mr. Kuzak's very door at the bottom, and the resultant methodical investigation and punishment made him briefly notable to his housemates, until they concluded that he was strange.

This was the final, the unbearable affront; they thought him strange, undisciplined, an inferior little boy given to pettish tantrums. He would show them; if there was one thing he was sure he possessed, it was a capacity for self-discipline. If there was one thing he would not be, it was a clown, a butt. He knew there was a certain dignity in his bearing, even though it shaded into pomposity, and he would not violate that, he would not become a Fruitcake Putsby, even if people would like him better that way.

He decided, in the season when the last leaves were drifting down from the trees bordering the playing fields, and the sunlight cut obliquely across the town, that there remained this one quality on which he could rely: his capacity for self-discipline. He would turn his back upon the school and the way things went there; he would no longer be embroiled in Devon's cheap competition for importance. He would be intelligent; yes, he told himself, he would be exceedingly, *exceedingly* intelligent; and by God, if he only could, he would be the greatest athlete ever to electrify a crowd on the playing fields of Devon. The greatest, and the most inaccessible.

The earth was turning wintry; boiling water simmered around the radiator handles in the dormitories and houses, the season of Steam Heat arrived. It filled every inhabited room in the school, the steam hissed and clanged with power, and could not be shut off. At night masters and boys would twist and strain at the radiator handles when they were ready for bed and had opened their windows a crack, but the power could not be excluded. All night steam whistled in thin, insistent jets into the rooms, and in the mornings the masters and boys would hurriedly release it lest this vast force grow furious and ex-

plode them all. Slowly the heat drained the spirit
from them, dried their healthy faces, seared the fresh-
est skin. The usual number of colds were contract-
ed and passed around, the usual amount of force
faded from lectures and application from homework,
the usual apathy slipped into the school through the
radiators. Winter was here.

Lawrence moved from one steaming box to another, crossing the sharp, dryly cold outdoors in
between, and felt his own inner strength grow as it
waned in those about him. He had in fact a stronger
character now, although it was the strength of the
season of Steam Heat, of pale faces and insistent
wills. He had learned to study very systematically
and his responses in class were apt and laconic,
several of his teachers became noticeably interested
in winning his good opinion; they would make remarks about Kafka or Turgenev and then glance at
him. He would smile back knowingly and resolve to
find out who these people might be.

His free time he spent watching athletics, reli-
giously following the major sports. During the first
few months he had watched football games and football drill, enjoying every moment except when Captain Marvel made a really brilliant play, which made
him feel uneasy and guilty. He watched soccer and
track and tennis and squash, and as winter sports
replaced them, he watched basketball, wrestling,
boxing, hockey, and even fencing.

In the fall he had played a little intramural football, at which he was generally inept and abstracted,
but once in a while he would startle everyone, in-
cluding himself, with a brilliantly skillful play. But
there was too much freedom on a football field, too
much room to maneuver, too many possibilities, so
in the winter he turned to the pool where the lanes

were rigidly predetermined and he had only to swim up and down, up and down. Into this he poured all the intensity he possessed, and as a result made the junior varsity squad, which was, of course, not nearly as important as being on a varsity team, but it was something. He was uniformly co-operative with his teammates, and the coach thought him a promising boy.

His housemates now felt disposed to revise their opinion of him; yes, Stewart was strange, but if he was going to turn out to be not only bright but also something of an athlete, they thought they had better accept him.

Acceptances of this kind are bound to be embarrassing when they follow a period of open mutual hostility. The proctor and the others made a few fumbling, gruff overtures. Lawrence sensed this at once and became more thoroughly disturbed than at any time since the dinner at the Inn. He loathed them all, of course, and he felt cheated; now that his defenses were invulnerable they were calling off the assault, inviting him to talk terms, asking for a conference out in the open. The dry cold tore around the angles of the old house, and Lawrence camped in his steamy room, speaking politely to those who came to the door, doing his homework, and feeling confusedly vindicated. He had proved the strongest of all, for what was strength if not the capacity for self-denial? He had divorced himself from them so successfully that now he didn't care; *they* cared, so it seemed, now; *they* were seeking his friendship, therefore they were weak. Strength, Lawrence was sure, was the capacity for self-denial; life was conquered by the strong-willed, success was demonstrated by austerity; it was the bleak who would inherit the earth. Yes, that was right and he would not allow them to change the rules now that he had won; he decided to continue his triumphant game, even though he was playing it alone.

Only in his anger did he draw close to them; one dismal afternoon in February, Billy Baldwin, the boy down the hall who had refused to room with him in September, came laughing to his door: "Hi, Varsity." This was the nickname Lawrence had been given by the other boys, who understood him much better than he thought. "You going to Bermuda for spring vacation?"

Since he was excluded from the gay round of parties which the boys from Boston and New York described as typical of their holidays, Lawrence had intimated that he was going to Bermuda with his family. This afternoon he was too depressed to lie. "No," he parroted with derisive mimicry, "I'm not going to Bermuda for spring vacation."

Billy was a little put off by this, but continued with determined good humor. "Well then, how about coming down, I mean if you aren't going home . . . " Billy had no champagne vacation in the offing either, but he had grown up a little during the winter and forgiven his parents for making their home in Bridgeport, Connecticut. He had also changed his mind about Lawrence, whom he now thought pleasantly temperamental and handsome. "Why don't you? If you want you could always—"

"What," interrupted Lawrence irritably. "Why don't I what?"

"All I was going to say," Billy continued on a stronger note, "what I was going to say if you didn't interrupt all the time . . . " but then he couldn't say it.

"You were going to say nothing," Lawrence said disgustedly, turning back to his book, "as usual."

"Just one thing, "Billy exclaimed sharply. "All I was going to say was, Why *don't* you go to Bermuda? If you're so rich!"

"Rich enough," Lawrence's voice thickened with controlled anger, "richer than some people who live in little dump towns on the New Haven Railroad."

"Yeah," Billy shouted, "yeah, so rich your pop couldn't pay the last bursar's bill on time!"

"What!" screamed Lawrence, tearing the book from his lap and jumping up, "Wha'd you say!" his blood pounding because it wasn't the truth but so close to it. He was standing now in the middle of his little garret, his shoulders slightly forward. His voice turned gutturally coarse, "Get out." Neither of them knew his voice had a savage depth like that. "Just get outta my room"; then in a single motion he snatched the book from the floor and hurled it at Billy's head. Billy sprang back from the doorway just in time, deeply frightened, not so much of him as with him. Both of them stood panting on either side of the doorway while several moments screamed past their ears, and then Billy went back to his own room.

Lawrence pretended to be totally unconcerned about such flare-ups, which occurred several times during the late winter. He eventually allowed Billy to re-establish a civil relationship with him. *After all,* Lawrence reasoned, *he should be the one to make up, after the way he insulted me right in my own room. I never did like him,* he reflected with a strengthening satisfaction, *no, I never did.* Billy didn't matter to him; in September, when he was so alone, Billy could have helped. But not now; what good was Billy? He was no athlete, no star, he did not possess that unconcerned majesty, he was a person of no importance. And Billy, who was just finding out about kindness, looked regretfully elsewhere for friends.

Except for these explosions, Lawrence maintained his admirable outer imperviousness throughout the piercing cold of the winter. He spent spring vacation in Virginia with his family. It was an uneventful two weeks except for a bitter little fight with Janine. "You're changed and I hate you," she cried at the end of it, and then, indignantly, "Who do you think you are, anyhow? I hate you!"

He returned in the middle of April to find Devon transformed. He had forgotten that the bleak lanes and roads, winding between gaunt, skeletal trees, were beautiful when the earth turned once again toward the sun. Tiny leaves of callow green sprouted from the gray branches, and the living scents of the earth hung softly in the air. Windows which had been stuck closed with the soot of winter were opened to allow the promising air to circulate freely; the steamy dryness of his little room drifted away; when he opened the single window and the door, a tantalizing breeze whipped across his papers and notebooks, fluttered the college pennants on his wall, and danced impartially on to the other rooms where his housemates stirred restlessly.

Then, unexpectedly, he began to slip in his studies. For two successive French classes he appeared unprepared, and when called on to discuss the lesson, he fumbled badly both times. The others in the class, to his deep humiliation and chagrin, snickered behind their notebooks. But the boy sitting next to him, with whom he had had a relationship consisting only of "Excuse me" and "hard assignment, wasn't it?," nudged him in the ribs as they were going out after the second class and exclaimed robustly, "Boy, did *you* stink today!" Lawrence was about to coin some cutting rejoinder when the boy grinned broadly. "You were really lousy," he added, punching him again. Lawrence tried and failed to keep from grinning back, and then muttered that, well, it was spring, wasn't it?

That afternoon he went as usual to watch the varsity lacrosse team practice. His own intramural team was having a game that day and could have used even his unsteady stick, but he had wrangled a medical excuse. Varsity lacrosse was almost as meaningful for him as varsity baseball, and he didn't have to watch Captain Marvel there. So he sat alone on the empty bleachers and followed the practice shots intently, watching the careless skill of the players, marveling at the grand unawareness with which they played. *This is the best part of the day,* he thought, *this is wonderful.* He pondered the assumptions on which these athletes operated, that they would not miss the ball, that if they did, they would catch it the next time, that their teammates accepted them regardless, that there was a basic peace among them which could be taken for granted. Lawrence could take nothing for granted; *yes, this is the best part of the day,* he told himself, and as he watched the skillful, confident boys warming to the game he saw only himself, he watched the others but he was seeing himself doing all the skillful, impossible things. He looked very pleased. *This is the best,* he thought, and despair flamed up in him.

He decided not to stay for the whole practice, and wandering back to the gym, he met his own team coming out; "Hey, Lawrence, get dressed"; "There's a game, Lawrence"; "C'mon, Stewart"; "What-thahellaryadoin?" The one thing he had wanted to avoid that day was his own team. Lately he always seemed to be stumbling into the very situations which he wanted fervently to avoid.

"Yeah," he called lamely to them, "but I got a . . ." Medical excuse? An Olympian unable to take the field because of sniffles? It wouldn't do. "Yeah, okay, I was just . . . the varsity . . . I thought maybe if I watched them . . . " To shout complicated explanations was impossible. "You know," he yelled, even though they were moving away, not listening, "I thought I might learn something."

"Forget the varsity, Varsity," one of them called over his shoulder, "the second-string Red midfield wants you."

This, then, was the afternoon when Lawrence scored his first goal. He felt an odd looseness playing that day, the hot rays of the sun seemed to draw the rigidity out of his body, leaving his muscles and sinews free to function as they would. Something about the way he held his stick was different, he found himself in the right place at the right time, his teammates sensed the change and passed the ball to him, and in the last minutes of the game he made a fast, instinctive turn around a burly Blue defenseman and scored the winning goal with a quick, sure shot.

It was a minor triumph which calmed his spirit for approximately seven minutes, until the invitation to the movies was issued and turned down, until he crossed over the little arching bridge, observed the water where his heroic reflection had shone, and stepped onto the turf on the other side, the varsity field. By the time they reached the gym it was Lawrence the unrecognized Olympian again, Lawrence the unknown and unloved.

After his shower he dressed and went, as he so often did, into the trophy room for a pacifying moment of dreaming. He knew the inscription and most of the names on the Fullerton Cup by heart, and in the space below "1951—Robert Graves Hartshorne" he would visualize "1952—Charles Taylor Morrell," for unquestionably the cup would be Marvel's this year. And the list should go on and on, with one celebrated name after another (even perhaps "1954—Lawrence Bates Stewart"), but here reality always intervened. The fact, the shocking fact was that the front plate of the cup was almost filled. After Marvel's name had been inscribed, the list would reach the little silver relief statues around the base—the old-fashioned football player looking slim and inadequate, the pompous baseball player with his squarely planted little cap, and the others—and there would be no more room. Nor was there any space to start a second list, since all the remaining circumference of the cup was devoted to an etched allegorical representation of the flame of knowledge passing from hand to hand through the ages, until it found its way into an elaborate device at the top of the back face, a coat-of-arms of birds and Latin and moons which was the seal of Devon.

Always a little amazed at this finiteness of the cup, Lawrence backed thoughtfully away from it. Wasn't this the core of everything, didn't it sum up, absorb, glorify everything at Devon? Yes, of course it did. And still, the cup would be full this year. One of these days it would be moved to a case along the walls with the other old trophies which had once reigned in the niche, it would be honorably, obscurely retired. In his imagination the heroic list stretched back over cup after cup into the past, and forward, upon cups not yet conceived, into the future. It was odd, he thought, all these great names fading into the past, getting less important every year, until finally they must just sort of go out, like the last burned-out ember in a fire. It was sad, of course, but, well, there was something almost ... almost *monotonous* about it.

Lawrence squirmed. He had never thought about the passage of time before. It made him feel better to realize it now, to see that the circle of the years changed things; it wasn't all up to him personally. Puzzled, he gazed around this chilly and deep chamber which had seemed so cool and serene in February, untouched by the bone-chilling winds outside or the rasping steam in the other rooms of the school.

But now it was April, and with the season of Steam Heat dead, Lawrence felt and saw April everywhere. He brought April with him into the trophy room, its freshness had touched his skin, its scents were in his clothes. This room isn't a chapel at all, he thought with a passing wave of indignation, it is a crypt.

Then, right there in the trophy room, he yawned, comfortably. And stretching his legs, to get the feeling of cramp out of them, he strode contentedly toward the door, through which a segment of sunlight poured down. As he stepped into it he felt its warmth on his shoulders. It was going to be a good summer.

Lawrence never knew that he was right in this, because he drowned that night, by the purest accident, in the river which winds between the playing fields. Bead and Bruce tried to save him; the water was very cold and black, and the night moonless. They eventually found him, doubled-over among some rushes. He had not cried out when the cramp convulsed him, so they did not know where to begin searching, and after they found him it was a hard, clumsy job getting him to shore. They tried artificial respiration at first, and then, becoming very frightened, started for help. But then Bruce thought again and came back to try to revive him while Bead ran to the gym, completely disrupting the movie in his frantic search for a master.

There was a conference two days later, attended by the headmaster, the dean, Mr. Kuzak from Lawrence's house, Bruce and Bead. The boys explained that it had been just a lark; students always swam in the river in the spring, and although they usually waited until it was warmer, they had decided in the Butt Room on Saturday night to have the first swim of the season while the rest of the school was at the movie. Bruce and Bead had planned it alone, but Lawrence had been there, very enthusiastic to go to the movie. Then when he heard they were going swimming, that had become the one thing he wanted to do.

"You know, sir," Bruce explained earnestly to the dean, "he was a good swimmer, and he wanted to go so much."

"Yeah," Bead confirmed eagerly, "we didn't ask him to go, did we, Bruce?"

"No, he just asked if he could and we said yes."

Bead set his face maturely. "He wasn't a very good friend of ours, but he just wanted to go. So we said okay, but it wasn't like we planned it together. I didn't know him very well, did you, Bruce?"

"No, I didn't either."

Mr. Kuzak studied the backs of his hands, and the headmaster asked, "Who were his close friends?"

"I don't know," Bead answered.

"The fellows in his house, I guess," said Bruce. Everyone looked at Mr. Kuzak, who thought of several perfunctory ways of confirming this, but knowing it was not true, he was unable to say anything. It had been easy to write "Stewart is beginning to find himself" on a report to the dean when Stewart was alive and could be heard trudging up the stairs every day; undoubtedly he *would* have found himself. But now the boy was dead, Mr. Kuzak had seen his body, had telephoned his parents; he said nothing.

Irritated, the headmaster leaned out of his throne-like chair. "He *had* close friends?" he persisted.

Still Mr. Kuzak could not speak.

"Well," the dean broke the uneasy silence, his kind, mournful eyes studying the two boys, "well, how did he ... was he," his fingers searched the lines in his forehead, "he enjoyed it, did he?" The dean's face reddened, he indulged in his chronic cough for several seconds. "He seemed lively? I mean, did he act ... happy before ... before this cramp seized him?"

"Oh sure!" Bead exclaimed. "Yes—yes, he did," Bruce said at the same time. "When we first got there," Bruce continued, "he got up on the bridge. Bead and I just slipped into the water from the bank, it was awfully cold."

"I never was in such cold water," Bead agreed.

"But Stewart got up on the bridge and stood there a minute."

"Then he dove," said Bead.

"Dived," someone corrected abstractly.

"It was a real dive," Bruce added thoughtfully, "he did a beautiful dive."

It had been like the free curve of powerful wings. Lawrence had cut the water almost soundlessly, and then burst up again a moment later, breaking a foaming silver circle on the black surface. Then he twisted over on his back and sank out of sight.

"I believe he enjoyed the water," said Mr. Kuzak quietly.

"Yeah," Bead agreed, "he liked it a lot, I think. That was the one thing he did like. He was good in the water."

"I don't think he cared," Bruce remarked suddenly.

The headmaster straightened sharply. "What do you mean?" Bruce's thoughts doubled over this instinctive statement, to censor it or deny it, but then, because this was death and the first he had ever really encountered, he persisted. "I mean in the dive he just seemed to trust everything, all of a sudden. He looked different, standing up there on the bridge."

"Happy?" asked the dean in a very low voice.

"Something like that. He wasn't scared, I know that."

The conference ended shortly afterward, with everyone agreed that it had been a wholly accidental death. A photograph of Lawrence in his swimming suit, taken when he made the junior varsity team, was enlarged, framed, and hung on the wall of the gym among pictures of athletic teams. He stood very straight in the picture, and his young eyes looked directly at the camera.

But the season moved on; that summer was the most beautiful and fruitful anyone could remember at Devon. Blossoms scented the air and hung over the river winding quietly through the playing fields. And the earth, turned full toward the sun, brought forth its annual harvest.

Summer
Street

There were trees forming a kind of nave over Jackson Street, a wide, still street which had been named for President Andrew Jackson. It was paved with gray, orderly bricks of an almost indoor quality. Along the edge, where the bricks met the low white curb, there was a strip of tar which became soft in the summer and formed little bubbles. When something broke the bubbles, they opened almost with a sigh to reveal brilliant black insides. Breaking bubbles was about as much violence as could be noticed on this semi-southern West Virginia street in summer.

Melvin Dorrance lived there. He was not quite old enough for sex and other complicated yearnings to have broken in upon him, and so he lived as though inside one of those bubbles, a cozy, covered-over life where everything was shiny. Winters were less shiny than summers, since then socks had to be continually pulled up straight under the elastic of corduroy knickers, and every day was ruined by school, which took the best part of it, and when school was over, the day almost immediately and very unfairly began to fade away. But when summer came and school very co-operatively stopped, the days even more co-operatively lengthened and lengthened, and the trees sent leaves climbing raggedly up to the peak of the nave again.

The one thing that bothered him this summer—aside from the trouble his dog, a sort of semi-wolf, had got into from attacking women who wore fur coats, but like all other troubles that went away in the summer—the one thing that worried him was where the new little sister his mother had gone to St. Louis to get was going to sleep. He knew it all had to do with sex and his father, but it was going to happen in St. Louis, and when his mother got back she would be not one person but two people and where was the other one going to sleep? His mother and father had one bedroom (he'd been over all this dozens of times but kept repeating it like multiplication tables), his older sister had her room, his older brother had his room, the colored maid, Yourenia, had her room downstairs, he had *his* room, and that was all the rooms to sleep in that there were. Babies slept practically all the time, and he had a suspicion he had not voiced yet, not quite even voiced to himself yet, that because this new sister would sleep more than he did, she might have a right to his room. And then where would he sleep? By the furnace? In the room where they kept wood and apples? On the back porch next to the garbage cans? Or was he going to be crowded out altogether, and have to go away somewhere? Where would he go? To New York? But if he went to New York, by himself that way, where would he find a place to sleep there?

He thought quite a bit about his new little sister; she was going to be "real cute," according to Mrs. Clue, who kept house while his mother was away. Everyone seemed to agree it was going to be a sister and not a brother because that would make the family even. Melvin, however, knew that they were not absolutely sure, and so he continued to hope for a brother. You could beat up a brother after a while, as his own brother had thoroughly demonstrated.

This new arrival was the only problem he had that summer. Just whether he was going to be thrown out into the streets or not. It seemed to him an entirely plausible problem, like the dog's trouble with fur coats. Having an unruly dog or facing the world alone, these were problems boys normally had.

One other limitation, not problem, on the shimmering joy he expected of any summer involved his friend Philip, who lived up the street. Philip had been forbidden to imagine anything any more. His mother forbade it. "No more pretend games," she suddenly ordered one day, after overhearing Mel and Philip elaborating for hours in her basement an extremely eventful story in which one of them was the King of Mexico with a gold mine and ten million head of cattle, and the other sometimes a rustler, sometimes Tom Mix, and sometimes a hopelessly untrustworthy Indian chief. She did not give the order in front of Melvin—she was too shy for that—but the next day and from that day forward Philip was forbidden to imagine. Neither of them had suspected that this was a bad thing to do, but it made as much sense as most other prohibitions, and so Philip stopped pretending. His mother would allow him to play real games, and he tried to substitute those with Mel—acting out running for President, or going to church, or dinner—but they were either failures or else exploded quickly into imagining, at which point Philip insisted they stop. They found that it was an impossible line to hold, and so they stopped playing any games at all.

Mel pretended, richly and elaborately, luxuriously, by himself in the backyard among some thin young trees. For example, he pretended that their house was much bigger and that this little grove was one of the rooms, the end room, in a new wing. The trees in his imagination were posts with glass doors between them, forming an irregularly oval room with glass walls. This was to be his new room. No room he had ever seen was as beautiful. These many-paned doors with their gilded frames looked out on vistas of park—the houses for a quarter of a mile or so around would have to be leveled to make the park—and there at night he would lie in a round bed with the darkness all around and just this glittering room of his alight, Wolf on the floor, and the radio playing music from New York. Sometimes, when she was older, he would allow his little sister to come over from his old room, where she would be trying to sleep, with its tin roof and two little windows, and visit him briefly in his glittering glass palace. Then she would have to go back, crying, to her cubbyhole, and he and Wolf and the radio would stay there together.

But if that didn't work he would have to go away, and that thought, it had to be admitted, was almost as gloomy as if Philip's mother herself had conceived it. He could not picture how days were spent anywhere else. Here they were so bright, all of them, so bright with something more than the sunshine. He didn't know what it was, but he felt it everywhere. Days began with breakfast in a little room off the kitchen, where the table and the chairs were shiny, and the window was open to the morning air sweeping in smells of the grass outside: he wanted to rush out so badly that it was an ordeal staying in the cool chair long enough to finish breakfast. And when he went out at last, there would be the morning hanging over the yard and street like a bright mesh with bits of mist caught in it. As the morning wore on, this veil would slowly be eaten away until by noon the street stood out as though all its lines had been traced with a paring knife, and all the colors of the leaves and shrubbery and flowers were deeper and more vivid than ever. Then there was lunch, in a big, cool, shadowy room with white curtains swirling in its big open windows, and ferns in dark-brown wicker trays. This particular summer, because his mother was away, Mel had these meals alone; his sister had been sent to relatives in another town and his brother to Boy Scout camp. Mrs. Clue was one of those stout old ladies who didn't seem to eat, and his father was only at home for dinner. He had lunch in the big cool room by himself, surrounded by the curtains rocking slowly above the ferns.

Many afternoons he took hikes. Philip was not permitted to hike because his mother felt it might make him dissatisfied with the neighborhood where he lived, and Mel therefore hiked with another friend, Sunny Ashcraft. *He* could go anywhere any time at all. There was no mother. Sunny lived with his father in a hotel near the railroad station. Mel had seen him once and been puzzlingly reminded of the high school boys he knew, because Sunny's father drove his car so fast and his face was so excited and in general he had a nervous high-school hilarity, only in his case it was blurred and redder.

Sunny came by Mel's house one afternoon of that silent summer and the two of them set off on a hike up the river. Sunny was fairly tall and his light-blond hair stood up on his head in a couple of big hooplike curls. He always wore brown gym shoes laced up over the ankles, and shorts, and some kind of shirt or other. They went together up the street through the summer stillness, crossed over a few blocks, feeling just slightly odder as they advanced into unfamiliarity. Mel's eyes narrowed slightly and his face became a little set. In Sunny's walk there was a certain up-and-down lilt, as though he had to sight their position with each step. They had made this hike before, but the terrain and the landmarks—the Esso station, the Methodist-Episcopal church at Tyler Street—were known to them but not familiar, not family-familiar. They crossed over the presidential streets, which ended without notice at Buchanan, since a Lincoln Street was not quite possible here, what with the Daughters of the Confederacy meetings and things like that. After Buchanan Street there was just a gravel road or two, and the boys veered off toward the river.

The river glided slowly between steep banks, a smoky, murky, metallic green river in a hollowly reverberating, steep little valley, crossed at a bend a short distance upstream by a railroad trestle. There were two passenger trains a day, one in the morning and one in the evening. Mel thought that he would take the evening train if he had to go to New York because it had a buffet car attached to the coach car. He had seen the train in the station and noticed that there were people sitting around drinking coffee and Cokes and being friendly in that buffet car; somebody might take an interest in him if he sat around there, and then this person might fix it so that he wouldn't have to go as far away as New York.

There were only these two passenger trains, but there were many others carrying coal; crossing the trestle, they might easily meet one. Still, there were two tracks on the trestle and a wooden walkway between them, so even if two coal trains began to cross it at once while they were on it, they could just keep walking along the walkway and be perfectly safe. They understood that theoretically. Mel had privately decided, however, that if even *one* train came boiling toward him on that rickety crisscross, all that careening metal hurtling shrieking down on him, he would get down on the walkway and lie flat on his face until it was past and all its noise was past. That's what he would do. He didn't know what Sunny would do. He didn't know what he would say, either, and he didn't care. *He* was going to lie flat on his face.

They started across the trestle, and through the network of rails and beams they could see the lazy, deep-green river passing underneath them. A faint sound, a far wail, could, it seemed to Mel, be heard from somewhere far up the empty valley. He glanced briefly at Sunny to see if he heard it. Apparently not; he was loping along in his explorer's walk, not seeming to hear anything like that wail, or whistle.

"Do they have coal trains on Saturdays?" Sunny said a minute or two later, stooping to re-tie a lace on his shoe.

"I don't think they do," said Mel. "Maybe."

Sunny was certainly getting far down to tie that lace; it seemed he was going blind, the way he had to get his eyes so close to it. He was leaning his head over to look at it sideways; then Mel noticed that in that position Sunny's ear was right next to the rail. You could hear trains coming a long way off by listening to the rail.

"My shoe's untied too," Mel murmured.

"Oh, is it?"

"Um-hum." Mel bent down on the other side of the walkway and gradually got his ear next to the other track. He listened; he listened absolutely. He heard the water swishing around the supports of the trestle, and he heard the river itself, which was silent, but still he heard it—the sound of movement, of water going past; he heard the distance between the trestle and the water. But he didn't hear any faint *click-click-click* of a train moving along the rails far away.

Neither, it seemed, did Sunny, because he stood up and looked at Mel just the way Mel was looking at him: a suspended, completely open look, everything completely wiped off his face, so that anything and everything he saw on Mel's could be taken in. Not seeing anything, any more than Mel saw anything on his, he said, "Gettin' hot," and began to take off his shirt. Mel took off his too, and they both tied the sleeves around their necks, and that made them feel even more confident than the endless silence along those silvery steel rails going all the way out of sight behind the hill of the far bank.

"Pop went up here two nights ago," Sunny said. "He musta gone right across this bridge. He went— you know where he went? He went to New York!"

Mel didn't even change his breathing, but he quietly filled up with consternation. There was no reason for this feeling, which made it that much stronger. Just because Mr. Ashcraft had gone to New York, what did that have to do with him? But that didn't quiet him; his fear grew. So he had to go to New York, after all. It was a sign, it was the fatal crack in the sidewalk and he had stepped on it, it was the short part of the wishbone, it was the first star of night and he had not seen it in time. Mel carefully preserved his silence for several minutes and then he asked, "Where's he stayin' in New York?"

"The Waldorf-Astoria Hotel," said Sunny immediately.

"Quit kiddin'. Where's he stayin' in New York?"

"How would I know!" Sunny suddenly burst out; Sunny hardly ever burst out that way.

"Well, you'd know because he's your father."

Sunny went along looking down at his gym shoes. "I don't know," he grumbled. "He's stayin' some place up there."

"Could you find out where he's stayin' up there?"

Sunny thought that over. "No," he said after a while.

Well, maybe Mel would run into him. It was possible. But he doubted it. New York was the biggest city in the world. There wouldn't be much chance of running into him. "Why can't you find out!" he then said, getting mad himself. "He's your own father!"

But Sunny had lapsed into his usual dreaming calmness. "Yeah," he answered, "but he runs around. He's not like some other fathers. I don't know. Maybe he *is* at the Waldorf-Astoria Hotel. He likes hotels. That's why our—we live in the Station Square Hotel. He likes hotels." He bobbed on a few more steps. "Me too."

"It's nice," Mel said, which was a mistake because it was too far from anything either of them could pretend to believe.

"You ain't even been in there," Sunny grumbled, his rare anger stirring again, saying "ain't" to make his protest stronger, to disfigure the way he spoke, to disfigure himself. That was how strong his resentment against the hotel and everything about it was; it made him want to disfigure himself.

Mel hadn't been inside the Station Square Hotel. He only knew that it rose at the foot of a steep gray hillside, and that it was grayer than the hillside. The coal-burning engines going by across the street next to the river threw up gray balloons of smoke which drifted over the hotel. Day and night, coal trains went through, first the big pulsing engine, and then car after heaping car, each clamoring nervously against the other as they went by.

Mel had always merely thought when in that neighborhood: there's the Station Square Hotel; that's where Sunny Ashcraft lives. Now, because of Sunny's sudden temper and because of that "ain't" Mel thought more deeply about the hotel, its anonymity fell away and he realized how gray it was, how much noise there was, how the sunlight probably couldn't get in through these smoked-up windows. He even visualized what a room inside would probably look like: pale dregs of grime-sifted sunlight falling on dirty white wallpaper, a rumpled gray-sheeted bed, clammy wooden floor, dark corners, emptiness. At the end of all these reflections he turned to Sunny and said, "Why don't you move?"

Sunny's mind had been going right along beside his, so he answered, "Pop likes to live downtown. I told you. He likes to run around."

"Yeah, but why don't *you* move?" They were just at the end of the trestle now, the awful passage was over. If a train came along now they could move off into the hills rising on all sides. The relief brought a burst of recklessness from Mel. "Why don't you run away?"

"Run away?" Sunny repeated vaguely. "Naw, I'm not going to run away."

Disappointed, Mel turned away from the tracks and headed into the country.

On this bank of the river the abrupt hills quickly blocked out the town and the railroad, and the boys were surrounded by high banks of trees; they came to sudden little bottomlands cut by funny creeks running along them, only to disappear underground and come restlessly up again, the grass here a kind of semi-mossy velvet; from ledges on the hillsides, thin metal streaks of water fell straight to the floor of the narrow valleys. It was very quiet but full of a sense of motion, from the thin plummeting streams, the broken hills, the weaving, disappearing streams. They picked their way across the bottomlands and through clefts in the hills, and saw no one until they came to a narrow orange brick road going straight up a steep hillside and into the hamlet of Melkville. There weren't many people visible in Melkville, either, and there was nobody at all again as they got beyond it along a high ridge from which they could see their hometown, the river, and the trestle, as frail looking now as a web. All this disappeared as they descended the far side of the ridge, through brambles and thickets and clusters of high weeds, where there were sudden hurried rushes now and then as small wild things got out of their way. The great open hillside undulated downward and they felt suddenly little here, short-legged, worn out by the sheer expansiveness of all this sloping land. It seemed as though they couldn't get anywhere, they felt themselves on a treadmill, dreaming, measuring a desert with toothpicks. A breeze starting a long

41

way off riffled slowly across all the high grass and then at last came sighing and whispering toward them and past them, disappearing in lazy riffles around the hillside. That was about the only visible movement anywhere as they made their way, wallowing through all this openness, downward toward the river, which had made a big U around the end of the ridge.

Very tired and slightly wounded, they broke through a final cluster of bushes, slid down a carved-out side of the bank, crossed the railroad tracks, which had stayed with the river as it circled the ridge, and reached the river itself.

There was a flat, warm dull-yellow rock next to the bank. They flopped down on that. They didn't say anything or do anything or look at anything for a while. Finally they revived, and quickly taking off their clothes, they ran into the river.

The spash and their voices echoed up and down the cool ravine. The water quickly supplied the antidote to all Mel's afflictions—fatigue, sweat, a sore knee, a scraped forearm; all of these infirmities were lifted away from him just as the weight of his body was by this very cool and very green water, all except one: the inescapable threat of the overfull house, the disputed room, the bleak buffet on the evening train to New York.

They paddled out to a rock near the middle of the river, Bubble Boulder it was called. There were deadly currents eddying around it, and it was inhabited by numerous poisonous snakes. Everyone knew this, although no one had ever been caught in a current or seen a snake. Mel and Sunny knew about both menaces, but they always swam, very frightened, out to Bubble Boulder.

They climbed its jagged sides and sat down on it. The distant cry of a whistle echoed toward them down the ravine. It gradually became louder, merging into the gray, hissing grumble of a coal train coming along. Then, with a blasting explosion, the train burst into sight around the bend; gray and black and steam-tossing, it boiled along the hillside. The engineer, sitting with his elbow clamped in the window of the inferno he drove, gave them a wave with his free hand; and after him there came a long, a very long hiss and clatter of coal cars. The engineer was long out of sight, forgotten, in the next state, and still they came hissing and clattering by, tossing noise back and forth roaring from one wall of the valley to the other, and making the two boys, perched precariously in the middle, in the midst of whirlpools and snakes, dizzy from the vibrations clanging over them. Then into view there suddenly shot the caboose, red as a carnival, frightened and frivolous, a damsel dragged along by this beast; someone was in its window also and exchanged waves with them. Then the caboose was out of sight, and the valley around them gradually began to subside, the quivering walls settled slowly into permanent place again, the river ceased its racing, groups of weeds regained their composure, fish resumed normal swimming, Bubble Boulder was found still to be in place, and Sunny said in a voice of ridiculous thinness, like a cricket on a battlefield, "You want to swim back?"

That train sure did make a racket, Mel was thinking; it just tore apart everything he liked here. I'll bet, he said to himself, bitterly, that that's the train from St. Louis. "You ready?" he said to Sunny, and evading snake holes they went to the edge of Bubble

Boulder, sprang holding their noses into the middle of the death-dealing whirlpools, and side-stroked to shore.

The long hike home was a dreary one for Mel; the day and his energy and everything else were fading, so that when they reached Buchanan Street it was all he could do to make it across the last blocks, across Pierce Street and Fillmore Street, Taylor Street, Polk Street, Tyler Street, Harrison Street, Van Buren Street, and to Jackson Street, home, at last. Home.

"Where you been?" Mrs. Clue started in the minute he got to the kitchen. "Your dad's been hunting for you all over."

"I been up the river."

"Well, he was put out, I can tell you. And now he's gone and you missed him."

"Where'd he go to?"

"Why, where *would* he go? He went to St. Louis. Something's going to happen any minute now over in St. Louis." She got pleasanter, wagging her finger at him. "He's going to come back with your ma, and something else."

"I know he's comin' back with something else!" He stalked out onto a little screened-in back porch off the kitchen. "You have to keep on all the time? Everybody *knows* there's going to be something else! I heard you before!"

She reared back and spread one hand over her bosom. "Well, aren't you something!"

"Yes! No!"

The next days passed in a state of suspension and, therefore, in a relic of happiness. There was, after all, breakfast in that bright room, there was lunch among the shadows and ferns, there was the silent street arched by the immobile leaves, and the soft tar with its bubbles, there was the mist in the morning and the knife clarity of noon, and then the still afternoons lazing by; there was Philip for reality and Sunny for illusion; and every evening, usually not long after Mrs. Clue had forced him to bed, there was a lone high hoot coming up from the river and the tracks, sailing across all the presidents from Buchanan to Jackson and coming lonesomely into his bedroom—for it was still his these nights, after all—and just kind of ending the day for him on a reminder that this one could be the last.

Mel wasn't wasting these last days entirely. The day after his father left he asked Philip to go to New York with him: he knew it was hopeless, but there was no harm in asking. At least it gave him an opportunity to discuss his flight with somebody. Philip not only refused but was frightened by the mere fact of having been asked, not frightened for himself, since it seemed to Mel that Philip never for a second considered doing any such thing, but frightened to be involved with anyone who would do any such thing. Philip just fell back a step and said, "No," hollowly, looking a little sick to his stomach, and he wouldn't even promise not to tell anybody that Mel was running away. They had a short fight over that, although Mel realized that Philip was at least showing the strength of honesty, the honesty to admit that if his nervous mother with her nervous glasses asked him if he knew anything about Mel's disappearance he would tell her everything, and at once. Mel noticed that Philip had no separateness at all; he was like one of those dolls who automatically blink when you hold them in one position and cry when you hold them in another.

He asked Sunny to go too, in spite of the refusal during the hike. Sunny had always gone anywhere any time. Mel couldn't quite understand why Sunny wouldn't even think about this. Se he went to see him at the Station Square Hotel. Sunny had never asked Mel nor anybody else to visit him there, but this time Mel went uninvited and found Sunny in his room. It turned out not to be his room exactly, because when his father went away Sunny wasn't allowed to stay in the two rooms with bath which they had. These rooms went back to the hotel to rent and Sunny was put in a very small room next to the elevator. "It's a service room," Sunny said, looking away from Mel as he came in. It had one window near the ceiling and no light came through it.

This seemed to Mel a favorable place to ask his question. "Well then, why don't you go to New York too, with me?"

Sunny slowly shook his head, as though trying to clear it. "Naw," he said, and when Mel argued with him and tried to say, without actually saying it, that he wouldn't be losing much, Sunny just kept saying, "Naw," and shaking his head. "There's a cat I always feed, across the street," he said, and "I'm playing basketball on the team next fall, there's nobody for center but me," and most strangely of all, "I like it here."

"Don't you want to see the world?"

"No." He didn't say his usual flat "Naw" this time, but "No," clearly and definitely.

"Why don't you?"

"There's nothing to see. I want to stay here." He went over to a cactus he had in a pot on a small table next to the bed. "There's nothing to see."

So there it was. Nobody was going to go with him. The baby was born the day after Sunny's refusal; it was a girl, all right. That day Mel talked to his father on the phone, said he was fine, and learned that the baby was as long as two panels on the glass door between the dining room and the hall. After he hung up he blocked out two panels on the doors with his hands. Not very long. A whole room for something that size? Well, it just proved where he stood if something like *that,* about as long as three Clark bars, could put him out.

Mrs. Clue said something the same day the phone call came from St. Louis about "the nursery." She said, "I guess your ma'll have to find a room for the nursery some place," in a thoughtful way, letting Mel just overhear what she was thinking. "One of the bedrooms, I guess. You two boys don't need rooms of your own. You could move in with your brother, for instance. That would be one way . . . " Her voice trailed off. "None of my business."

"In with my brother! He won't even let me *walk through* his room, did you happen to know that? How'm I going to sleep in there!"

Indulgent, preoccupied laughter from Mrs. Clue. "Oh, huh-huh, you boys, fussing, always a squabble, nice big room . . . " She put some clothespins in her mouth and went out the back door with a basket of wash.

His mother called long distance a day or two later and he talked to her for a little while. She sounded the same. Then she asked him to give the phone to Mrs. Clue for a minute. He stood behind the glass door in the dining room, his hand on one of the panels, and overheard Mrs. Clue say "Yes" in the half-surprised way she had, and "I see just what you mean," and "Why, it's just as easy as anything!" and then she hung up and said, "Yes, we're just going to change things around a little bit upstairs, just like I figured. You'll have that nice big room with your brother, and we'll put little sister in that little corner place where you are. Just right. Come on, give me a hand," her voice leading away up the stairs, "big strong boy."

Mel followed her up the stairs, and wordlessly began helping out in the dispossession of himself. Putting the family crib in the middle of the room was not so bad, and he didn't particularly mind setting up a frail miniature bathtub next to the window, but stripping the walls of his pennants, emptying drawers of his clothes, evacuating his collections of stamps and matchboxes from the desk made him feel light-headed and bereft. There was a risqué picture book he'd pondered and puzzled over in a kind of hazy excitement—Sunny had found it in his father's closet and lent it to him—and the recollection of that, secreted inside a shoe box inside a suitcase behind a large empty carton covered by an old curtain at the back of the closet, suddenly struck him. The sun was washing into the oblong little room with its sloping ceiling, the white curtains were lifting and falling, and Mrs. Clue was approaching his closet, exclaiming, "Now we'll just scoop up *all* of this and put it right where it belongs in the other closet."

"Mrs. Clue!" he cried.

She stopped and turned. "Well?"

"Mrs. Clue," he thought of and rejected a half-dozen interruptions—that he had a sudden pain in his stomach, that he had just heard the doorbell, that he kept his snakes in the closet—and then he said, "The closet is my personal place."

She settled back a little, looking at him, and then said not unkindly, "Oh, I see. It is, is it? Then you'll want to clear it out yourself." She went off with the neckties into his brother's room.

But that was his only victory. All else that afternoon was sweeping, abject defeat. His own room, which had been his all his life, stripped of every trace of himself. His things had been moved into the next room, but nobody could move the pattern thrown by the shadow of the curtains on the wall, nobody could uproot the big tree which spread itself outside his window and whispered vague messages to him all summer long, whispered stories about the sea, for instance, and about love, a lot of sighing messages he could not make out about love. Nobody was going to move the tin roof outside his window, where a *rat-tat-tat* marched him to sleep every rainy night, and where in a real downpour wild herds seemed to stampede. Well, but what did any of that matter, the tree or the tin roof or anything? What really mattered, what blinded him in a strange way, was that his own mother had ordered him out of his room and into a room where she knew he couldn't stay, since his brother, who was bigger, wouldn't let him. She'd put him out of the house, in other words. Damn her! *Damn* her! He started to pack; his things were scattered all over his brother's room, so it was the perfect time to start. He threw some clothes into the small suitcase on top of the strange and stirring picture book of Sunny's father, went out the back door, and started walking toward the station. He would be in plenty of time for the evening train. He had nearly sixty dollars from various birthday gifts and other sources, and he knew the ticket for New York was much less than that. The stationmaster did not know him, so he didn't see why a boy who was no longer childish-looking wouldn't be sold a ticket.

It was nearly a mile walk, and the suitcase got very heavy toward the end. He set it down at the edge of Station Square, and then he saw Sunny going into the hotel. Sunny saw him and came over. "You going?"

"Yeah. Why don't you come? I got about sixty dollars." Sunny looked slightly stunned when he named this sum, but clung to his decision. "C'mon," Mel urged anyway, "c'mon."

"I'm going to wait for my pop to come back from being away. I have to be here."

"Why?"

"Well, he thinks I'm going to be here, that's why. He expects I'm going to be here."

But Sunny seemed to mean more than he said. Mel read minds of course, other boys' minds especially, and he realized that Sunny believed that his father not only expected him to be there when he came back but counted on his being there, depended on it, needed for Sunny to be there. Mr. Ashcraft, Sunny believed, needed his son. What a peculiar thought.

He picked up the bag again and the two of them crossed the square to the station. They went down an iron stairway to the track level, and Mel went up to the window, behind which the man did not look up, and said, "One ticket to New York, New York, please."

The man looked up then, an elderly, skinny man with glasses and a green eyeshade. "New York, New York?" he repeated, squinting to see better or because he thought something was funny.

"Yes."

The old man looked him over a little, and then he said, "One way or round trip? First class or coach?"

"One way," said Mel immediately, because that was the kind of finality this trip had, and "Coach," because that's where the buffet car was.

"That'll cost you fourteen dollars and seventy-five

cents," the man said without making any movement to indicate he was preparing a ticket.

"Well, I have fifty-eight dollars and five cents, so I could even take the Pullman. But I want the coach. One way. New York, New York."

The man sighed briefly, and then pulled out a long yellow strip of paper and began filling in blanks on it with his pen. "What you going to do up in New York, boy? Visit somebody?"

"I live in New York. I'm on my way home. From Arizona. I was in Arizona before, and then I stopped here, and now I am going home to New York."

"Sure have a mountain accent for a New York boy," said the man, looking up again and stopping his writing. "Where'd you get that talk?"

"I used to live here before. Then we moved to New York. That's why I came back. To visit my grandmother."

"Uhmm," the man muttered, and returned to filling out the ticket. He stamped it several times, Mel paid him, and then he and Sunny went to sit on his suitcase in the corner of the station. Several other people drifted into the echoy room, and then the far hoot of the train whistle came sailing down from the ravine. It shriveled Mel's spine; he shot up from the suitcase, cried, "Do you think that's it," knowing it was, and then the incredibly high black screaming engine, hooting and roaring, more and more overpowering, forced itself into the rocking station. It stopped and seemed to sink with an immense, hissing noise, and after a minute or two someone hollered " 'Board!" and clutching his bag, Mel headed toward the chancy warmth of the buffet car with its possibly friendly occupants and then he heard Sunny say, "There's your *father!*" and he quickly scrambled onto the steps of the buffet car, because not only his father, but his mother as well, holding something which must be his sister, were descending from the Pullman car at the rear of the train. They looked the same as they always had, even with this baby, and wasn't it funny, he suddenly thought, that Sunny was staying to meet his father when he came home, his father who never gave him a nickel, never watched him play basketball, never bought him a soda, never did *anything* for him, while he himself was not going to be here to meet his own parents, who until now had done quite a few things for him. That was funny, and it was even funnier that Philip wouldn't even consider leaving, when you thought of what *his* mother was like. Then he began to feel ungrateful, which was the one thing he couldn't stand feeling—" 'Board!" somebody yelled down the platform again, and he saw his father and a porter go past, just below where he stood on the platform of the buffet car. He just wasn't as good as Sunny and Philip were, that's all there was to it; if you were good you did what you were told, no matter how they treated you. And he knew in his heart that he would never be good, couldn't be, didn't want to be. Let Sunny be, let Philip be. He himself was going to have to be bad. His mother went rather slowly by, carrying his sister. Maybe she had another plan for him that he himself hadn't thought of; maybe she did plan a new room or a wing or something to build onto the house, and his staying in his brother's room was only temporary and would be okay with his brother until this new room was built. He didn't know for sure; maybe she did. Maybe they had thought of him and how he was going to live with them, after all. He could not know for sure until he saw what they did. The train was trembling preliminarily, and before the conductor could put down the metal flooring blocking the stairs, Mel stepped forward with a feeling like a tight knot in his chest and throat and went down the stairs.

"Hey!" he yelled, although he realized that finding him at the station with the suitcase would reveal all his evil to them. But he couldn't do anything else; there they were, they were his and he had to catch them; he would rather be revealed in his crime than not catch up to them. Sunny turned around in surprise, and Mel thought what loyalty boys like Sunny and Philip had, and his own baseness assailed him again. "Wait for me!" he yelled after his parents up the platform. They still hadn't heard him, and as he trotted along he tripped over his bag and fell to one knee, which hurt. "Why doesn't she wait, damn her!" he grumbled to himself, and kept on going.

The
Peeping Tom

One hot July night in the town of Wetherford, Connecticut, Mrs. Marion Carver, a widow who supported herself and three children comfortably by selling insurance, stepped onto the small back porch of her home wearing only a nightgown and a housecoat, to put out the milk bottles. There, just outside the screened-in porch, backed into some evergreen shrubbery, stood a man, his eyes glittering in the light from the half-open kitchen door, staring at her. She had heard about the Peeping Tom who was infuriating the town. He didn't move, and through the woman's mind flashed the sensation that she would not ever move again. Then he began to back deeper into the trees, still staring unwaveringly at her, and every tiny rustle of the shrubbery thundered in her ears.

"Go away!" she cried in a much too frightened voice. He moved out of the shadows then, and for a second of incredulous relief she thought he would be gone. But he halted before her, with only the fragile screen between them, and even in that moment she was able to think, How young he is! even as he leaned toward her, his shoulders hunched, his eyes immobile upon her as his head swayed faintly back and forth. His jaw was clamped shut, as though in terrible resolve, and then he jerked it open, almost convulsively. "Fool," he swore at her, "ugly, stinking whore!" but the shock of it was mitigated for her because a moment later he was gone around the corner of the house and only his voice still hung in the air, deep and surly, but edged with the croak of adolescence, like her son's. Mrs. Carver put the bottles in their usual place, went back into the house, and hesitated several minutes before calling the police.

It was an unacceptable news item and the Wetherford *Weekly Newsletter* did not carry it. The fifteen thousand residents of the town all habitually leafed through the paper and did not expect to find such a story there; printed in words on paper, it would become too real, and no one wanted that.

Outright violence was something else, and the *Newsletter* had headlined the town's one murder in recent years. But a Peeping Tom; somehow it was more outrageous than murder—so tentative, so misty and obscene, it hinted of mysteries better hidden behind sanatorium walls or locked in psychiatrists' files, better left subterranean and unexplored. For all the residents of Wetherford maintained balances of one sort or another, and this Peeping Tom balanced too, teetering between desire and fear; it was best that they should not read about him.

A Peeping Tom, terrorizing this respectable town, glimpsed by solitary matrons darting across their lawns, seen for one horrifying instant at a first-floor bedroom window—he was in a sense more offensive than a murderer, never assaulting, holding back in his own ominous balance. It was too much a grotesque parody of normal lives.

It was not printed in the *Newsletter* but it reached

58

every corner of the town, passed along in those electric whispers which fixed it, more deeply than headlines, in every mind. Husbands stayed at home nights, and children, overhearing fragments of the tale, immediately introduced The Man into their make-believe. Sometimes he was a villain, whom they shot at from windows and trees; sometimes he was the avenging phantom meting out justice on his nightly rides.

Many of the women lived on the verge of hysteria. Several confessed that they were incapable of sitting in a room at night without all the blinds drawn, and a few learned to load their husbands' revolvers and declared to their friends that they would shoot the monster on sight. The more timorous of them slipped into bewilderment whenever the subject was mentioned, and gazing about dazedly, would murmur that, well, it was just like war, too horrible to discuss. But all the wives joined upon one policy; it was up to their husbands, even more than to the police, to protect them from this menace.

So a loosely organized vigilante committee was somewhat reluctantly formed to patrol the area around Broad Road where the peeper had most often been beheld. It was late June and hot, and the men, shirt-sleeved and sweaty, protected their homes ill-humoredly, moving with plodding, unathletic gait up and down Broad Road and the side streets leading into it. They carried flashlights and clubs, and their white shirts, looking a little indecent without coats and ties, shone through the night half a block before them.

They never saw the peeper and they found no clues which might reveal anything about him; but they learned something about themselves. They seized a high school boy trying to get into his home late at night without waking his parents, they flushed a drunk and several cats from a vacant lot, they gave chase to milkmen. After ten days or so of this, such discipline as there was, crumbled; men failed to report for duty and those who did often crept home, in the emptiness before dawn, to snatch a short nap on the livingroom couch during their duty hours. Naturally they did not want their wives to know this, and one of them, stealing in through a basement window, was seen by a sleepless neighbor who raised an immediate resounding alarm.

Soon the vigilantes, trying as they were to fight fire with fire, found themselves falling into disrepute throughout the town. A rumor circulated that they were frequently drunk on duty; people began complaining that they were just as alarming and far more numerous than the peeper.

It became clear that they could not play, let alone fight, with fire, and they began insisting to their wives that the Wetherford police department, feeble and understaffed as it was, would have to deal with the situation.

A final, acrimonious meeting was held. A rising young lawyer appeared and presented a thoroughly systematized, highly complex plan of reorganization. There was to be a carefully graduated hierarchy and efficient liaison with both local and state police, there were provisions for zones, signals, field headquarters, subcommittees, equipment requirements. "I have faith in this," the lawyer declared to them, moved by his accomplishment, "I know if we just tighten up our organization," he hesitated and then banged a table with his fist, "tighten up our organization, we can catch this nut." The others said they had faith in it too.

Still, they raised a variety of objections, rather petulantly: the plan required too many people, not enough people; it relied too much on the police, the police were not doing their part; time was wasted on detail, yet it was not detailed enough. Toward midnight agreement was finally reached that the plan was unworkable, the vigilante movement impracticable, the existence of the peeper open to question. They voted to disband and went home. When their wives would sigh and complain at them, a proper response was, "Oh, come on now, dear, he isn't going to bite you."

But the day after Mrs. Carver saw the Peeping Tom at such close quarters, it was all over. She was able to give the police a good description of him and he was picked up at his home. He was a tall, rangy young man, loose-jointed and, at first, very talkative. The extreme politeness of the arresting officer toward his mother and his wife made it seem as though he were co-operating in catching someone else, some criminal. As he left, with his family leaning in the doorway, the woman livid, the girl bewildered, he waved encouragingly from the window of the police cruiser, to show them that this wasn't anything, for it seemed that it wasn't.

The young man—his name was Paul Marowski—was told that he was charged with breach of the peace. Still, he remained friendly until they entered the police station—a gray-walled box with two glass-enclosed offices, a plain counter across the front of the main room with desks and radio equipment behind it, and large maps like nerve X-rays hung about the walls, uniforms, badges, and rumbling voices—entering the station silenced and tightened him. His jaw set and he looked moodily at the floor.

He was given a chair next to the clerk, who began recording his vital statistics on a form sheet while behind him police officers moved about. But there was something routine about their activity and voices which relaxed him, and when the chief of police began a boisterous description of the Fourth of July parade to the detective sergeant, Paul Marowski seemed to feel safe again, for this wasn't anything, couldn't be anything if people were joking. In fact, the detective sergeant was growing uneasy and embarrassed at this levity by the chief, whose habit was to remain rather aloof from the rest of the force.

"Age?" said the clerk.

"Twenty-four."

"But this fat guy," laughed the chief, "this muddlehead, shoved out right in front of the goddamn band . . ."

"Height?"

"Ah—well, I guess five eleven, or maybe eleven and a half."

"You're employed?"

"Yeah—yes, I am. At the Wetherford Machinery Company. In the warehouse."

The chief's story was very successful; staccato laughter bounced through the little station, and the prisoner, who had been watching the clerk closely as he recorded the statistics, half turned around, beginning to smile, although he had missed the climax of the story. The laughter subsided, and the chief, after a moment's hesitation, turned and walked heavily into his office. From there he called to the clerk. "Fingerprints, Mr. Peters," he said rather formally.

"Yes, sir, we'll get those." He turned back to the prisoner. "You were in the service?"

"Yes."

A pause. Mr. Peters, his pencil poised, turned a little impatiently back toward him. "Well, what branch?"

"Oh," breathed the young man. "Oh, sure. I was in the Air Force. Let's see . . . I enlisted."

This seemed to interest the detective and the officers standing around. They listened sociably, and although the clerk wrote very little of it down, no one interrupted as he described his service career: Texas, Alabama, Illinois; no overseas; discharge; a normal tour of duty. The prisoner even felt confident enough now to indulge in a digression, a story of a leave in Chicago during which he lost his pass and had to elude the military police at every turn. The clerk volunteered a smile, and several of the officers chuckled. The chief came to the door of his office, and leaning comfortably against the jamb, listened too, while seeming to study a piece of paper.

"You got back, did you," Mr. Peters murmured, "without getting caught?"

"Yeah," grinned Paul Marowski, "I got back okay after all."

The clerk turned back to the form sheet, reread what he had written there, and finally asked without emphasis. "Are you willing to make a statement at this time?"

"A statement?"

"Yes. A statement. On what you have been doing, on this—on your breach of the peace."

The prisoner looked away from the clerk and stared confusedly up at the others. "What kind of a statement," he said faintly and rapidly, "I don't see what to say, what could I say on this?"

The chief straightened in the doorway. "It is your

63

prerogative to make no statement if you don't wish to, this is only if you would want to make a full admission of guilt now."

The young man could not seem to bring the chief into focus. He squinted across at him. "You mean I should confess, make a statement confessing?"

"That's correct."

He turned quickly in his chair, and grasping the arms of it, leaned out toward Mr. Peters. "I don't get that," he said with rising inflection, "I don't get that at all. What kind of a statement of guilt? I don't see that at all. Why should I do that, why do I have to do that?" he had turned away from Mr. Peters, and these last words were directed across the room, at the big man in the doorway.

The chief came over to him rapidly for such a heavy man, and fixing his large hands on the arm of Paul Marowski's chair, demanded, "Why were you looking into the windows at Mrs. Carver's last night? Why did you stand on the lawn at the Marvins' house for half an hour on July second? Why were you outside the bedroom window at 268 Broad Road on June twenty-seventh? Why have you been seen eleven times in the last two months looking in windows, in women's windows?" The other men stared expressionlessly at the prisoner.

With each accusation the young man appeared to lose some of his confusion, to become, more and more as the demands broke upon him, aloof from his surroundings, as though he were gradually ceasing to hear what was said to him. "What do you mean," he replied at last in a careful, fluent voice which quavered just noticeably, "when you say 'Why?' "

"Why? Why?" exclaimed the chief in brusque surprise. "Why were you there, what were you doing there? What do you think I mean?"

"Oh, that's what you mean," he said quickly, "you want to know 'What?' "

"Well, well then, 'What?' What were you doing there?"

He wanted facts. That was different. The young man began with a description of how he looked into a window for the first time last June, what he saw, what he did; he tried to describe how he felt at the time. At the beginning of the statement Paul Marowski's very mouth revolted, the words came out maimed and twisted, like a foreigner's. Every few seconds he had to stop for breath, since he suddenly had forgotten how to breathe naturally. But by the time he finished he was talking very rapidly.

These facts fulfilled the requirements of the police. An officer typed them as they were given, the chief went back into his office, and Mr. Peters moved up to the counter across the front of the station, to record a traffic violation.

Paul Marowski assumed that they would lock him up after he had finished the statement, but instead they set his bond at two hundred and fifty dollars, and although he suddenly had no desire to be free at all, he called his home as they directed. Jeanie soon appeared, accompanied by his mother, to post the money. Mrs. Marowski remained in the background during this transaction, clutching her purse to her bosom, as though she feared being robbed at any moment. Her gray hair was more awry than usual, and under her colorless face, which looked moldable like dough, her facial bones were set indignantly. Paul Marowski could not watch Jeanie counting out the bills to Mr. Peters; her thin arms seemed so emaciated, so childlike that he was afraid they might suddenly lose the power of performing such an adult skill as paying bail money, and twine girlishly

65

around her head. He wondered where they had raised the money, and then he wondered why.

His mother, who drove very rarely, insisted on driving their battered Chevrolet home, and again, although she was a very talkative woman, did not speak as they drove along. This could mean only one thing, and Paul Marowski and his wife began the nervous dialogue which this kind of silence always forced on them. They discussed feeding the baby, watering the lawn, he said he would shave and then go to work, although he was already late, and she suggested that they go to a movie that night.

"There's a good movie at the Palace," Jeanie exclaimed and floundered forward into a description of what she thought was the plot. They both began discussing it with extreme interest, their comments curving in under each other to catch the conversation each time, to bear it up again. Mrs. Marowski said nothing. Jeanie became almost shrill in her praise of the film's stars, Paul Marowski cross-questioned her closely on details.

Mrs. Marowski was driving fast and awkwardly, shifting gears unnecessarily, racing the motor.

"I think movie stars memorize their lines before each scene," Jeanie was saying, "don't you think so? I mean, I don't know, I think they'd have to, don't you?"

"Sure," he exclaimed, "sure, I guess they must. Unless they read them off blackboards or some way like that."

"Maybe if we watch this movie tonight real closely we can tell."

He started to agree with her, and since his voice was resonant, it drowned out a sudden expletive from Mrs. Marowski. He stopped speaking instantly.

66

"What is it, Mother?" Jeanie asked in a faint voice.

"Yes, do!" Mrs. Marowski blurted out, her eyes narrowing. "You two go to the movies! Just right," her voice grew fiercely sarcastic, "you two go to a movie!"

Mrs. Marowski stopped in front of their house and stepped out, and Jeanie slid over to the door to follow. "But, Mother," she said, "you'll be going to your Social Star meeting tonight."

Mrs. Marowski gazed back over her shoulder. "Of course I have resigned from the Star," she pronounced, almost drawled.

But as soon as she had slammed the front door behind her, she crumbled over into sobs, stumbled forward into the living room, sobbing deep, parched sobs. "Oh Paul, oh Paul!" she cried through her hands.

Mrs. Carver did not want to testify. The police had told her that since Marowski had given a statement, he would almost certainly plead guilty in court, but she should be there, just in case. She had never attended town court, but she knew that it met in a little school auditorium and she had always imagined it as slightly comic. It had never occurred to her that a case of these dimensions could be tried there; stop-sign violations, yes, even perhaps a minor theft; but a Peeping Tom? It didn't seem sensible or even legal. She wanted to stay at home with her sons, she did not want to see this boy again. She did not want to hear his voice, with the echo of adolescence in it. But she went, demurely dressed, and sat in a folding chair in the back row.

Paul Marowski entered alone a few minutes later

and slipped into a seat across the aisle from her. "Well, there he is," said Mrs. Weaver in a hollow whisper to Mrs. Carver, elbowing her husband at the same time. "There he is, Phil."

Phil Weaver leaned across his wife to speak to Mrs. Carver, a neighbor whom he always treated with a certain deference. "She gets all worked up," he said confidentially, indicating his wife, who looked both shocked and pleased, "she's been hollering for weeks about this."

"Well, I hope you won't mind if I tell you I was glad," Mrs. Weaver broke in with a low laugh, "when he came to your house instead of mine. I just know I would have fainted."

Mrs. Carver opened and shut the snap on her purse. "It really wasn't so bad, you know," she said sociably, and immediately hated the complacent tone of her voice, hated having to discuss the thing at all, especially in this way. "I just—you know, when I saw he was so young . . ."

"Young beast, if anyone should ask you," exclaimed Mrs. Weaver as though she were taking a dare.

Her husband grinned slowly. "A real operator, that guy, yessir, quite a big-time operator."

"Silly," his wife said to him. "You're awful."

Mrs. Weaver didn't think her husband was awful, really. Not Phil. Loud, yes. But not awful. She peeked over at the youth again. He was the awful one, with those mean dark eyes of his snapping at the room, and the way he clenched his long sinewy hands together, and his shoulders, she noticed they were wide, hunched menacingly forward. Isn't he awful, she reflected.

"Why don't we get on with this," Mrs. Weaver whispered irritably, "what could they be waiting for?" She fanned herself with a newspaper, for the room was filling up, mostly with young people in their teens, and becoming close and hot. Overhead, four-bladed fans licked the heavy air flowing languidly down upon them. The boys and girls, in bright shirts and dungarees or skirts, trooped down the aisle, slumping into strange, comfortable postures in the rickety chairs, and gradually surrendered their animation to the heat. In a space at the front of the room the little judge's bench, on a low dais, was solemnly empty.

Mrs. Carver looked at it. An unshaded lamp hung over it and there were other bulbs about the room offering bleak illumination. The heat and starkness of the place, and her own uneasy feeling of foreboding, were so like another time that she drifted into a hazy recollection of it, hazy at first, and then cruelly clear. Memories of the past usually bored her, they were a waste of time and her habit was to push them, simply and efficiently, out of her mind. But not this particular one, not this one because it flashed "Danger!" when it came, sprang into her mind with a threat, demanding total recall.

Let me think. When on earth was it?

The memory pushed against her, and Mrs. Carver turned at last upon it. All right, what is it, what is it?

It was of certain customs offices in distressed tropical states which she had visited years before, traveling with her husband; shabby port offices where natives who had fled from some violence in the interior would sit mute and motionless along the walls, waiting for the seals and signatures, the money and tickets which would open the door from them into the world beyond.

She had pitied them at the time, of course; who wouldn't? They were so impulsive and headlong, obsessed with a single thought: to run away and be free. Yet invariably in their obsession to escape they lost the means to escape, for they abandoned whatever job they had and plunged desperately away from the chaos in the back country, stole their way somehow to the coast, to the port of embarkation, only to wait there, helpless and without resources, for some stroke which would set them free into the world beyond, totally incapable, because of their paralyzing passion for freedom, to be free.

Mrs. Carver, young, smart, and immensely proud of her successful husband, pitied them but could not help scorning them, could not avoid thinking them inferior, when compared with her husband. She resolved to learn a lesson which she would pass on to the children she hoped to have: that they must be like their parents (of course, how could they help but be), smart, and ambitious. Whenever they were inclined to sloth or stubbornness she would tell them about these stunned, lost natives of the tropics.

It had been a temptation to judge the matter on a racial basis, and since she was a woman of liberal persuasion, she was relieved to encounter other natives who ruled out this judgment, who were wise and competent and got what they wanted. These too could be seen in the port offices, lately come down from the interior, where they had patiently, phlegmatically worked their way, year by year, up to authoritative positions on some ranch or mine or plantation, surviving the flashes of killing which would sweep sporadically over the countryside. Then, when the necessary money, seals, and tickets were assured, they would descend triumphantly to the port. Invariably they ignored and disdained even to glance at their staring, paralyzed fellow natives slumped against the walls; they knew this kind: the headstrong ones who rebelled against the insecurity of back country life and fled, with many a ringing defiance, to the coast. And doubtless they hated them, for it could not have been easy to stay plodding away at a job when others left with shouts of "I go to be free and happy. I have had enough of this suffering and fear."

Now was their moment of vindication and triumph; there along the walls, ragged and lusterless, were those rebels who had departed with such high hearts, and the new arrivals would carefully husband their baggage past them, steeled to flash out murderously at any interference. When all was carefully prepared they would set sail, out into the world of freedom and safety, leaving their fellows to stare hypnotically after the great ship as it dropped away over the curve of the earth toward freedom.

Mrs. Carver was delighted to see this, since it confirmed everything she had been taught. "You see, darling," she declared happily to her husband, "it's just an individual thing. It hasn't anything to do with racial inferiority. Some of them are good and some are bad, just like all other peoples. And it's up to the individual to achieve his destiny." It was a hot day and her husband had been trying to attract a porter for their luggage, so he had only muttered in reply something about, yes, he supposed so, and Mrs. Carver, who was a little self-conscious about her idealism and her flights of eloquence, rather forgot the idea.

It recurred, strongly, as she sat in the hot little courtroom, and it seemed a crude and dull concept: *Some of them are good and some are bad;* no, it wouldn't do, it broke down, fell out of its neat division, goodness and badness slopped together amid the chaos of her thoughts, because she had detected the adolescent echo in the voice of a Peeping Tom and it had sounded so like, so frighteningly like familiar voices.

How would her own son learn, she asked herself, very calmly because it was such an overwhelming question, to proceed circumspectly through life, never to strangle it, always to coax, to wheedle it; he must learn that life must be lightly stroked and gently urged along, as though life were an inscrutable cat.

The court officer, a pert young man seated at a table to the left of the judge's bench, suddenly stood up and banged his gavel. The spectators rose, shaking out their languor. A door behind the bench opened and the judge stepped out, thin, pale, and scholarly-looking. "Open court, Mr. Officer," he said softly, and the young man recited the call to order in a rapid, incomprehensible monotone.

"Oh, here we go!" whispered Mrs. Weaver in muffled excitement, as though they were starting a roller-coaster ride. But her enthusiasm quickly faded, for the prosecutor began presenting the stock town-court cases. "Your Honor, Mr. Barker here was arrested by Officer Stenhaus on July thirteenth on Route Number Seventeen. Officer Stenhaus says he clocked Mr. Barker at sixty-eight miles an hour from the Kenway Drive crossing to Newell Corners . . ." Mrs. Weaver returned to fanning herself with the newspaper which she had creased and folded like a real fan, and shielding her face with it, she would glance from time to time over at the intense young offender, that dark youth, Paul Marowski.

He was rubbing his temples with his left hand and drawing his fingers across his forehead, as though reading the thoughts within by Braille. Well, this is it, he said to himself, and why is everyone *looking* at me! There were several policemen talking desultorily along the rear wall behind him, and while the townspeople in the room all seemed to have accusing eyes and hate-filled hearts, the police appeared kind and familiar; he felt a quick warmth and liking for them. They all knew. They had listened to his confession (what a horrible word), his confession of guilt (he could not say this word clearly), and yet they were *still here.* They talked as they had done before, dressed the same, undoubtedly ate and slept the same. He had always dreaded that when people finally learned of his crimes they would immediately disintegrate, or turn to stone, or be struck dumb. His violations seemed so searing that all commonplaceness would vanish before them like snow in July. The police know! he told himself incredulously, and without warning, tears were forcing themselves into his eyes; they know, he cried with bitter relief, like lying exhausted in hot water after having been beaten and beaten; they know.

He must stop this. Think about something else. There was that Mrs. Carver sitting right across the aisle from him. He wasn't afraid of her any more, either. She had a very nice house, a very comfortable, homey house. He remembered the bright, somehow happy-looking hooked rugs scattered on the living-room floor which he had seen through a window that night; one of her kids had been sprawled on the floor, reading something. Paul Marowski had watched Mrs. Carver come into the living room carrying a dishcloth, say something to the boy, and smile. The boy had looked up and said something, and then turned back to his book. She stood over him for a moment, and then with a kind of absent-minded humor she dropped the cloth onto his head, moved back to the door and out of the room. The boy had gone right on reading, and after a minute or two he slowly drew the cloth from his head, and without taking his eyes from the book, he rolled it and folded it this way and that with his hand. To Paul Marowski, leaning awkwardly forward over a prickly bush, straining to see all yet be unseen, it had been like a dream, like some magic country where women and boys played humorous tricks on each other; where interesting books were read in safe living rooms, and where dishcloths were dropped in fun by calm, smiling women.

Well, it's probably a lot of fun, he thought, yes, I guess that would be a lot of fun. He never had to use dishcloths at home because his mother and Jeanie agreed that dishes were a woman's job. He was supposed to fix things, and when they didn't work his mother would say what a pity it was that Paul ("Paul" always meant his father at home; he was called "son" by his mother, and any number of endearments, but not "Paul," to avoid confusion, by Jeanie) had not lived long enough to pass on to his son his own amazing manual gifts. There was a radio, a large ornate instrument with doors, which Paul had taken apart immediately after it was bought in 1951 and then put back together again, improving so much on the work of the manufacturers that it "played beautifully, beautifully" his mother would remind them, to this day. Two years ago, just before he married Jeanie, he had thought to take the radio apart himself; he admired this skillful, cloudy father of his very much (what a wonder he must have been), and if only he could take that radio apart correctly, with infinite pains, tube by coil by wire—why, then somewhere in the mechanism, somewhere in the amazing perfection with which each piece had been related to every other piece, would be the gift he sought. He knew that such a plan wasn't logical, but this particular radio seemed such an extraordinary instrument that he felt sure there must be something somewhere within it which existed nowhere else. He would probe and figure and probe again, and then, when he had it all reassembled, fresh music would pour forth, and he would have learned something important from his father.

When he suggested this to Mrs. Marowski she had not looked up, but seeming to smile slightly, she had said, "Yes, why don't you?" in an unusually sophisticated voice for her, the voice she used when discussing one neighbor with another. But he hadn't; he unscrewed the back, and the mechanism, obscured with dust, offered no starting place, seemed so tightly integrated that it could not be broken down piece by piece but would have to be pulled violently apart, all at once. Hurriedly he screwed the back into place again for fear he had already gone too far and ruined it.

When Jeanie came to the house as his wife this search lost some of its intensity, it seemed that his hands had gifts of their own. It was only when their son was born that again he wondered and worried whether he had anything of real value to pass on to him. His mother wanted to name the baby Paul; Jeanie concurred, but he startled them both with the vehemence of his refusal. He liked the name Stanley, he insisted; it didn't make any difference that there weren't any Stanleys in either family nor that he had no friends named Stanley; he liked the name, that was all.

The house with the baby there was like a nursery upstairs and down. Diapers, formulas, bottles, odd new smells, rickety little bathtubs, cryings and feedings and rashes and sniffles. Every activity seemed directed toward the child, and Jeanie and his mother did them all; these were women's jobs. "You can have him later, when he turns into a little rough-neck," they said, "but now he's ours, he's a woman's job now."

Paul Marowski fell ill when the baby was six months old. It was diagnosed as overwork and he was housebound for almost two months, being tend-ed as well as these two busy women could manage. He felt wretched about this and fought mightily to be well. But some vitality had ebbed in him; under-taking even small odd jobs around the house ex-hausted him, and his eyesight, always very good, unexpectedly dimmed. He spent eight discouraging weeks in bedroom slippers padding uncertainly from room to room, trying awkwardly to keep out of the way.

Eventually the symptoms diminished and he re-turned to work, weakened and somewhat stunned, as though someone were periodically hitting him pain-lessly but jarringly on the head. His son was still in the efficient care of the women, and he could not think how to behave toward him.

I wonder, I wonder, he would say in his continu-ing interior dialogue, how my own father acted with me. One evening, when the baby was about a year old, he finally asked his mother about this. It was June and Paul Marowski was sitting on the porch steps while his mother was meditatively resting on the old porch swing. Upstairs he could hear Jeanie talking to the baby as she got him ready for bed. Mrs. Marowski waited so long to answer that he was about to repeat his question when she said, "Oh, he was always busy. He'd play with you a little and then, often as not, he'd go out. He was an active man, son, very active in things around town." And the reproach against him was there, worse because of the gentleness in her voice that night, worse and deeper and with an invincible sadness in it, as impenetrable as life or the big radio in the living room.

She creaked back and forth on the old sagging swing, very slowly and deliberately. Active man. The words sank into the rhythmic creak of the swing. Active man. Active ... man. Active, active, active man. This sound was not loud, it was deliberate and it was ceaseless; it had a draining quality in it for Paul Marowski; it was so measured and deliberate that he could not think how to stop it, forget it, ignore it; it progressed across him unemphatically, and stopped the impatient beat which he had been abstractly tapping on the wooden porch floor, stopped that and seemed to dim, then extinguish Jeanie's faint voice above, moving into unassertive control.

At last he started up, steadied himself against the banister of the porch and mumbled, "I think I'll go up and help Jeanie."

"No," Mrs. Marowski murmured without interrupting her dreams, "don't."

"Anyway, I have to go to the basement," he said, looking away from her. He was standing, shaky and disjointed-looking, in her line of vision, but she still saw, beyond him, something in the distance. He opened the screen door with caution and stepped inside. It took him a long time to close it again; it must not under any circumstances slam, for this would wake the baby, disturb Jeanie, and break into, crack open the flowing rhythm of the swing.

The basement was crowded with indoor clotheslines, a washing machine, racks, baskets of clothespins, washtubs. All women's facilities. There was also a neglected workbench and the old coal furnace.

In another hour he and Jeanie would go to bed. But it seemed unlikely that he would be able to do this tonight, in view of the danger of making some noise there, some spring creaking, some rustling of sheets. It would be a terrible mistake to risk being overheard there. Maybe she would come out with him, out somewhere else, in some field or river bank. But of course Jeanie was bound to this house, this home, this nest for their little son, little Paul. No! I mean Stanley! Christ. Yes, of course, Stanley. Stanley. Stanley. Stanley.

He was shaking, and leaned back against the cluttered workbench. The basement was dark, with only a little of the fading evening light penetrating through a grimy window over the bench (washing windows was a man's job).

The furnace, very big and black, was two steps away from him. One of his earliest memories was the pounding, housequaking thunder of his father shaking down the ashes in it. The furnace was like the spine of the house, and every night after his mother had put him to bed, his father would grasp this spine in his gifted hands and seem to wrench every board, every nail around him.

Then, and before he knew what was happening, Paul Marowski crossed to the iron handle of the furnace and meshed his fingers, one by one, very tightly around it.

With a great sigh he thrust it forward and then back, and the old roar started almost slowly, almost as though taken by surprise, up through the house. He jerked it back and forth faster and faster, and it didn't matter that he was crying because nothing could be heard except this deep, manly pounding, no other sound, and control of the house passed into his strong hands, where it was wrenched and wrenched and wrenched.

Sometime later he stopped, and left the house by the basement door. It was on that night that he became a Peeping Tom, and when he returned at about two o'clock in the morning he went straight to Jeanie's arms and lay there whispering his love for her most of the night.

Only, the freedom didn't last. Again and again the house passed out of his control; the windows stayed grimy, the workbench remained neglected. And through it the women moved quietly, tending the child. Paul Marowski at first would make an effort to help them, striving for a goodhumored and casual air. "I'll heat the formula," he would offer, smiling. But what size pan should be used, and would it be too hot, not hot enough? When he asked several such questions his mother often became exasperated and Jeanie knit her brows; finally he was forced out of the kitchen, and sprawling on the living-room sofa, he leafed, too quickly, through magazines. A few days of this and his strength left him again. Soon the wall between him and Jeanie would rise once again, and Paul Marowski had to beat it down somehow, to level it by an expedition at night, through trees and underbrush, a glimpse through windows, an outrageous sight; an activity of his own.

I know what I'll do, he thought, sitting at the back of the courtroom waiting for his case to be called, I'll take Jeanie and Stan and we'll go away, somewhere by the water. I'll make a boat and we can sail around in it, and whenever we want to . . . let's see, how about a houseboat, then we could just dock wherever we wanted to. That would be nice, I guess, wouldn't it? Maybe it wasn't possible, but wishing to be calm, he tried not to think of that.

"Paul Marowski!" the prosecutor called loudly.

"Well, at *last!*" breathed Mrs. Weaver. Her husband grinned. Mrs. Carver drew herself almost primly together: "Yes, at last." The room was impossibly hot, and she felt a detached surprise at the energy with which the young man walked forward to face the judge. There was a little humid pool where her shoulder touched Mrs. Weaver's, whose fan drove the heavy air dully across her face.

The prosecutor, a florid, balding man, touched the accused on the arm. "How do you plead?" he asked in a confidential tone. Paul Marowski started slightly. He had a choice of pleas, funny he'd forgotten that. Of course he was guilty. But it seemed awful to say the word, in answer to what he was accused of here. He began shaping it in his mouth, trying to produce it undistorted.

The prosecutor mistook his hesitation. "You can plead nolo if you wish," he said. Paul Marowski looked at him inquiringly.

"That's nolo contendere," said the judge helpfully, "no defense. You throw yourself on the mercy of the court."

How lurid! thought Mrs. Carver.

"Nolo," said Paul Marowski.

The judge said he could not accept this plea without hearing some of the evidence, so the statement which the prisoner had made to the police was rather dramatically read by the prosecutor. It was a straight recounting of facts, and since Paul Marowski did not know the genteel circumlocutions of law courts it contained words like "naked," phrases like "I got all worked up," and caused a sensation among the spectators. Mrs. Weaver's newspaper fan froze in mid-sweep and she held it there, transfixed, throughout the reading.

The young people found it powerfully stimulating, and the room became alive with their nudges and broad winks, the indolent atmosphere was charged with their repressed gasps and impulsive giggles. Twice the judge interrupted the reading to call for order, and as the prosecutor swept toward a new climax he broke in again, ordering the court to be cleared of everyone who was not an adult. The court officer began ushering out the young people and this touched off several little scenes, for they were a brash and self-reliant crowd. The prosecutor stood fanning himself with the confession, and as the front row emptied the prisoner sat down and put his elbows glumly on his knees. Gradually the room was cleared, leaving only a little knot of adults in the rear, and the court functionaries gathered around the bench. Between these two groups sat Paul Marowski, alone as though everyone had drawn away from him, alone beneath the licking fan, the naked light bulb, his chin sunk on his hands, reflecting, Anyhow, those kids heard enough, now they know too. He had been amazed at their rudeness to the court officer; he expected after what they had heard that they would rise like ghosts and float soundlessly out.

He stood up again amid the sudden silence of the place, and the prosecutor, unconsciously taking this as a cue, continued the reading, " 'My last time was last night'—that would be . . . let's see, July sixteenth, your Honor, the night before the arrest."

"Yes, yes. Continue."

" 'I knew about this Mrs. Carver and I wanted for a long time to see in her house. She was a good-looking woman but when I got there it turned out the bedrooms were upstairs and I just looked in on the living room. I saw one of her kids on the floor, and I saw her for a minute, but that's all I saw. I didn't scare anybody but I ran into her at the back of the house and I got very excited and scared but I don't remember anything that happened. I don't think I said anything but she might have screamed. I don't know. I just remember coming in the basement door at home later.' That's the entire statement, your Honor."

Paul Marowski's face was working and his hands were clenched behind him, digging into each other. For this was the worst moment of all. They know all about me, he thought desperately, they know it all now. This was his confession, and with the reading of it out loud like this, out in court, he was beaten again, heavily, officially, a beating not to be repeated; a beating such as this must necessarily terminate something, introduce something else. No one emerged unchanged from such a thing.

His face was contorted with this thought. Can this be it? The judge was listening to informal testimony from the arresting officer, and Paul Marowski was passing into that moment when it would be all over, the beating and outrage behind him, and intoxicatingly before him were the exhaustion and the used-up feeling, but most of all the freedom was advancing to fold him in her temporary embrace. I'm getting out of my trap, he thought excitedly, this judge and this court, they're doing something, action is being taken; nothing will be like before, I'm getting out of my trap.

Seeing that her testimony wasn't going to be required, Mrs. Carver hurriedly stood up.

"But wait," whispered Mrs. Weaver. "We've still got to see—"

"No. No, we don't. I don't."

I forgive you! she wanted to cry dramatically to him across the stuffy little courtroom. But of course that would have shocked everybody almost as much as the Peeping Tom had. Instead she walked quietly but quickly out of the courtroom and home to her sons.

Martin
the Fisherman

I went to sea one day with Martin the fisherman. It's complicated, arranging to go out in a Basque fishing boat. First one must consult with the *patron*, the boss; the *patron* agrees, for I am a comrade of Martin, and Martin makes the trembling little five-horsepower motor of the *Chingudy* operate twenty hours a day, five days a week, every week of the year. Besides, Martin would prefer to be a mechanic, and to work only eight or ten hours a day, and on dry land, so the *patron* is willing to make small concessions to keep him content.

But there are other complications—a visitor is expected to buy a liter bottle of wine for each man on the boat, and the *Chingudy* has ten. This would be a very heavy load for me to carry to the port at one-thirty in the morning when the fishermen go out, but there are ways of doing such things. The brother-in-law of the chef in my hotel handles wine and delivers it to the boats directly, strong, red Algerian wine for sixty-five old francs a bottle. I pay the chef eight hundred francs, he gives his brother-in-law seven hundred francs, the brother-in-law purchases the wine and hires a runner to deliver it to the *Chingudy*. Thus everything arranges itself.

There is one final formality. The *Chingudy* has no permit to transport passengers, and therefore the *patron* feels called on to protect himself. I write out a paper for him: *"Le patron du bateau* Chingudy *n'assume aucune responsabilité pour les accidents qui me pourraient poursuivre en mer. Fait à St. Jean de Luz, France 1 août, 1959"*; my signature at the bottom, and that of the concierge as attest. The *patron's* mind is now at rest; it is now only a contest between me and the sea, and he is but one who observes.

I arrive at the little port of St. Jean at one-fifteen in the morning, the Basque beret which I have bought for the sea planted confidently on my head, food for three meals at sea in a large box under my arm. The port is quietly busy at this hour. Boats pull up one after another at the stone steps descending from the quay to the water, and take on the great nets, the gasoline, the panniers of food and wine; and the *Chingudy* takes on one passenger, or, it is to be hoped, one more crew member for the day. The *patron*, in the tiny cabin amidships, steers with deliberation across the port and through the concrete-walled channel into the Bay of Biscay. The crew disappear into their bunks below decks to sleep until dawn. I am wrapped in a canvas tarpaulin and comfortably established on the rear deck, my wrist lashed to a gunwale. The sea is black, except for a glittering path of gold which the moon leads off to the coast of Spain. The boat sways back and forth; my hand has fallen asleep; I detach the rope from my wrist; soon I am asleep.

I awake in a strange, lifeless light. It is gray everywhere, a colorless gray full of empty shades: the sky is gray, the sea, the cabin amidships, the tarpaulin, my hands are gray. The sea is heavier, the

Chingudy plows on but rolls deeply, unevenly from side to side. Again I fall asleep. When I awake it has grown lighter, colors are distinguishable; two crew members are bustling near me on the afterdeck, preparing sardine bait. They are Pierrot, the auxiliary pilot who relieves the *patron*, and le Mousse, the little one. They are filling barrels with fish eggs and water and mixing them with both hands. Le Mousse is small but strong-armed, he mixes away lustily, his black beret bobbing up and down. Then there is equipment to be carried aft; le Mousse's brown feet pad rapidly back and forth, his eyes look out brightly from time to time at the waves from behind shell-rimmed glasses, his full blue Basque pants fluttering in the wind. His face is small-featured and tanned. In a dark suit and white collar he could easily be sitting in chapel at a famous school; he is sixteen.

"You have seasickness?" he asks eagerly.

"No," I reply. "Naturally not."

Pierrot is thirty-four and laughing; his ruddy face curves into a smile as easily as the sea curves into waves, he laughs at the American struggling out of the tarpaulin, he laughs at le Mousse sliding about the pitching deck, he laughs and makes faces at the back of the *patron*'s head. He wears a clean white undershirt and a pair of great yellow rubber pants. He has a little hammer and a little knife, and he is continually molding bits of metal to serve as sinkers for the net, or whittling at clubs to use for braining the great tuna we hope to catch. He smiles happily at me.

"You are sick?"

I am braced in a corner next to the cabin. "No, still not."

89

Martin comes up from below deck. He emits a deep, contemplative grumble. "You're sick?"

"No, I don't believe so."

He stands staring sleepily at the eastern sky, where hundreds of tiny clouds are suspended, red from the invisible sun. From the wide bottoms of his pants to the floppy beret perched on the back of his head, he is a Basque fisherman. He is lean and agile, with large, clever, blacknailed hands. His blue eyes slope down a little, and his wide mouth curves up, with a droll upper lip protruding in eternal amusement. His nose is long and just a little crooked, and his skin is always tanned.

The fishermen like to speak Basque, but because there is an American on board, they speak French.

"We had a Parisian with us last month," says Martin, "Pierrot's second cousin. He became very sick just about this time, just at dawn." The sun, deep red, is rising over Biarritz. The water suddenly is bright green and sparkling silver; two little rowboats are lowered into it with a fisherman and a barrel of sardine bait in each.

"There are many sardines here," he adds, "and when we fill the containers with sardines"—he gestures toward two large wooden tanks, fore and aft—"we will search for the tuna."

The fishermen row away in opposite directions, scattering bait as they go. We wait. Martin lies down on the deck; it is getting warm, he puts his beret over his face, he hopes to fall asleep. Le Mousse is busy mixing more bait; the *patron* stands alone in the little cabin, he does not speak to anyone, no one speaks to him. His wide, square shoulders remain stolidly motionless even when the *Chingudy* rolls hard. The other fishermen gather fore and aft for breakfast: bread, chicken wings, some ham, and an apple. They squeeze the gourd of wine and a thin red stream squirts into their mouths. I eat with them, and then I smoke a strong French cigarette.

"The cigarette will perhaps make you sick?" suggests le Mousse hesitantly.

"No, I don't think I will be sick at all."

The *patron* shouts something in Basque to le Mousse; he scurries forward. Some sardines have gathered; the *Chingudy* circles the two rowboats and we lower the net. If these sardines get away, we may spend the whole day looking for more, so everyone begins to work very fast.

By the time the net is in and the tanks are full of sardines it is very hot. The *Chingudy* rolls like a fretful sleeper.

"We have enough sardines now," says Martin, "now we go after the tuna." But suddenly I wish I had never heard of sardines, or tuna, or the *Chingudy*. I move evenly toward the side; I curse French cigarettes.

"Ah! You're sick," says Martin with interest.

We are farther from the coast now, the Basque beaches and cliffs stretch in a thin white line on the horizon. The sun has passed its zenith but continues to blaze down on the *Chingudy*. There is no time to eat chicken or drink from the gourd now; the *patron* and Mario, the Spaniard, are standing in the stern of the boat, feeding lines baited with glittering artificial sardines into the water. All around us the other boats from St. Jean hover intently. This is where the gulls have been seen lately to dive at the water for little fish, so this is where the great tuna are. The *patron* is a magical fisherman; almost the instant his line strikes the water a tuna snaps at it, and the *patron* never lets one escape. Behind him stands

Martin with a hook on the end of a long pole to gaff the fish when it is brought alongside, and next to him stands Pierrot with his ornate club, cheerfully smashing the fish above the eyes after Martin drops it on the deck. Behind them is the wooden tank of sardines, and le Mousse, standing on a barrel, has been dipping into it for five hours with a small net, drawing out sardines and flinging them over the heads of the fishermen, into the water, luring on the tuna. He seizes a small, jellylike fish by the tail and holds it out for me; I reach for it and he draws it away, laughing. "Be on guard against this little fish. It is a *vive,* and it can sting you and make you swell. Later it grows and is good to eat, but now it only stings," and he throws it over the side.

I watch him throwing the sardines as he has been doing for five hours. "Why don't you get a . . ." I do not know the French word for slingshot but I pantomime. Le Mousse almost falls off the barrel, he laughs so hard at this idea. The *patron* wheels around. "Throw!" he shouts and makes a threatening gesture with his free hand. He is holding a spare hook in it and the hook grazes Martin's shoulder, it tears a long rip in his sleeve. The *patron* glances briefly at him; Martin stares back, his wide mouth is now an even line. He opens the hole in his sleeve, but there is no cut.

"I will mend this," he says to the *patron,* and hands his hook to Pierrot. Pierrot mimics a seamstress furiously, using the hook as a needle. The *patron* turns back to his fishing.

There is a tremendous needle on board which was not meant to mend shirts, but it will do. I begin to sew up Martin's sleeve for him. "The *patron* is often excitable," Martin explains, "when it is hot and the tuna are striking fast."

"Certainly," I answer.

Le Mousse agrees. "He is very excitable, and he catches very many fish."

We are all uncomfortable from the heat. Martin takes up the gourd of wine and plants his feet wide on the deck, as though preparing to fire a gun; his head rises proudly on his strong neck, it seems to be in combat with the wine rushing into his mouth; he holds his shoulders back, his free hand on his hip. When he finishes he squirts a little into le Mousse's face; le Mousse sputters.

"He does not drink wine," Martin confides loudly to me behind his hand. "He doesn't like the girls either, all he wants to do is fish."

"You," le Mousse answers brightly, "you waste all your money on the girls."

"He's an infant, you know," Martin adds confidentially. "He thinks women only exist to buy fish."

Le Mousse finds this very funny, gaily he throws out another fish, but instantly he realizes it is going to fall short, he half cries out. Pierrot turns just in time to snatch the fish before it strikes the *patron*. Suddenly he starts, it is a *vive*. He jostles the *patron*, who is leaning over in concentration, bringing a tuna alongside. The *patron* cries out, catches himself, and does not fall overboard. But the fish escapes.

The *patron's* face is deep red under his deep tan. He roars a single word in Basque and pushes his hand, hard, into Pierrot's face. Poor Pierrot, who does not know how to behave in trouble, falls back a step, more embarrassed than hurt. Le Mousse leaps off his barrel and rushes to the *patron*. "No, no, *patron*, it isn't his fault, it's mine!" In his excitement he clutches the *patron's* sleeves.

"You are playing schoolboy pranks on my boat?" shouts the *patron*. "I work like a madman to make

93

some money and you make me lose my fish!" The crew watch mutely, the ocean itself seems silenced by his rage. Le Mousse still clings to his sleeves, but he is sinking down, almost kneeling. "I will not have you on my boat!" With a furious push he thrusts le Mousse against the gunwale, but suddenly it is the *patron*, not le Mousse, who hurtles forward and over, into the water. Martin stares after him with a look of concern. Then he pulls le Mousse back from his precarious perch on the gunwale.

After a moment the *patron* reappears on the surface. His beret sags over one eye. His mouth is open, but he says nothing.

"I am very sorry, *patron*," Martin begins rapidly, earnestly. "I hope you will forgive me, but everyone was getting very feverish. It was not le Mousse's fault that you lost the tuna. He has been throwing out sardines for many hours and he accidentally threw one short—I was disturbing him, the American and I, we upset him."

Mario, the Spaniard, lifts his palms toward the sky and opens his eyes wide. "It seems that all the world is at fault."

"We are sorry, *patron*," Martin continues, "we are all very sorry." There is a general murmur of sorrow from the crew.

The *patron* says nothing, but swims slowly, in a crablike breaststroke, up to the side. Twenty hands offer to assist him up. He ignores them all. With quiet concentration he hoists himself back onto the deck. He removes his beret and wrings it out, he thrusts a finger into each ear. Pierrot half offers the gourd of wine; the *patron* accepts it, he squirts a great stream of wine down his throat.

"Perhaps the American is right," he says at length, "perhaps if le Mousse had a slingshot . . . "

The sun is far away in the west, a wan crimson glow shows where it has gone; in the east stars, cold and beautiful, gleam in the deep-blue sky. Over Spain the exotic moon glitters down again, reflecting in the water a shimmering channel of light, down which we sail to St. Jean de Luz.

Phineas

I t was the kind of place I had expected all right, an old, rooted Massachusetts town. All of the homes along Main Street, from solid white mansions to neat saltboxes, were settled behind their fences and hedges as though invulnerable to change.

I approached a particular house. The yard was large but the house had been built close to the street. A hedge as high as my shoulder separated it from the sidewalk. I kept calm until I reached the break in the hedge and saw the marker. It was the name, in small, clear letters. I stood beneath an ancient, impregnable elm and got myself ready to knock at Finny's door.

Three months before, I had gone unsuspectingly to another door and first encountered him. The summer session of the Devon School convened that year in June, and when I opened the door of the room assigned me, there was Finny, standing in the middle of the floor and pulling handfuls of clothes carelessly out of a suitcase.

I had seen him at a distance around the school the previous winter and gotten the impression that he was bigger than I was. But when he straightened up, our eyes met dead level. For a second I thought he was going to say, "I'll bet my old man can lick your old man." Then his mouth broke into a grin, and he said, "Where did you get that dizzy shirt?"

It was like one of the shifts which made him so good at sports: exactly what the opponent didn't expect. I had been prepared to introduce myself, or to waive that and exclaim, "Well, I guess we're roommates!" or to begin negotiating an immediate, hostile division of the available floor space. Instead, he cut through everything and began criticizing my clothes —*my* clothes—while he stood there in hacked-off khaki pants and an undershirt. As a matter of fact, I was wearing a lime-green, short-sleeved sports shirt with the bottom squared and worn outside the pants, much admired in the South. "At home," I said. "Where did you think?"

"I don't know, but I can see that home is *way* down yonder." He had an unusual voice, as though he had some baritone instrument in his chest which would amaze you if he didn't keep it under control. You could clearly hear the music in it when he spoke: it was only when he tried to sing, which he often did, that music fled and his voice wailed off key ("Like an Arabian lament," the director of the Glee Club once commented).

Finny made me understand that we should be close friends at once. That first day, standing in our comfortless room amid his clothes, he began to talk and I began to listen. He wanted to establish a firm understanding on all subjects, so he covered the field, beginning with God and moving undeviatingly through to sex. "I'm not too bright about all this," he began, "and I don't understand much about theories, but the way it's always seemed to me . . . " and then he outlined his beliefs. I didn't like them much; they had an eccentric, first-hand originality which cut straight across everything I had been told to believe. God, he felt, was Someone you had to discover for yourself. Nothing important had ever been written or said about Him. Sermons were usually hot air; formal prayers were drill.

Sex was vital, and that was why it was surrounded by even more fantasy than God. He had experienced it three times, and gave detailed, completely matter-of-fact and unboastful accounts of all three, omitting only the girls' names out of gallantry.

"How many times have you slept with a girl?" he asked, fixing his interested eyes on mine.

I was supposed to take up my story at this point. But my ideas would have been as dull as a catechism after his; it seemed as though I had never had an original thought in my life. Besides, this wasn't the way we talked with strangers in the South.

I hadn't asked for all these confidences, and I wasn't going to give mine in return. "I'll tell you about it someday," I answered in what I thought was a cool, rebuffing tone.

"All right," exclaimed Finny with cheerful uncon-cern. "Will I be interested?"

"You'll be as interested as I was in yours." I liked the screened irony of this reply, lie though it was.

"Good!" He flung his empty suitcase into a cor-ner, where it landed at an angle against the wall and stayed that way for the rest of the summer.

I wasn't going to be opened up like that suitcase, to have him yank out all my thoughts and feelings and scatter them around underfoot. So he went on talking and I kept on restively listening through the first weeks of summer.

Finny declared himself especially pleased with this weather, but I found later that all weathers delighted Phineas.

For that was his real name, and it is important for two reasons: first, it was just the kind of special old New England name he would have, and second, no one ever thought to kid him about it. At the Devon School kidding people, or "cutting them down," as it was called, gave place only to athletics as a field of concentration. No one could be allowed to grow above the prevailing level; anyone who threatened to must be instantly and collectively cut down. But Phineas at Devon was like the elms I came to find in his home town, so rooted and realized and proportional that the idea of felling them was unthinkable. Not that he wasn't kidded: his amazing way of dressing, his enjoyment of singing and his inability ever to be on key, the score of fourteen he got on a Latin examination, his habit of emptying his pockets on the floor at night, the icebox he bought which wouldn't hold ice or water, his failure to realize that he was naked when he went calling around the dormitory after a shower, all of these habits were kidded endlessly. But not cut down; they were too exceptional for that. We searched for ways to get at him for a while and then realized that it was impossible, because he never forced himself up.

All of us were at Devon for the summer session, the first in the history of the school. It was because of the war, to hurry us toward graduation before we became eighteen and draftable. We sixteen-year-olds were brought back for the summer and our pace stepped up noticeably. It's odd that such a peaceful summer should have resulted from war.

We became a muted New England adaptation of gilded youth that summer, we boys of sixteen. The masters were more bénevolent toward us than at any other time. I think we relieved them of some of their pressure; we reminded them of what peace was like, of lives not bound up with destruction.

Phineas was the essence of this careless peace. Not that he was unconcerned about the war. On the third morning of the session he decided to wear his pink shirt, to memorialize the bombing of the Ploesti oil fields. It was a finely woven broadcloth, carefully cut, and very pink. No one else in the school could have worn it without some risk of having it torn from his back. But Finny put it on with the air of a monarch assuming the regalia. As he was buttoning the collar he at last acknowledged my absorbed stare, letting his eyes slide slowly from the mirror around to me.

"I figured it was a good day to put it on," he said stoutly, "on account of the oil fields." I just kept staring at him in mystification. "Well, you've got to do *something* to celebrate," he added rebukingly. "You can't just let something like that go by."

"Talk about *my* dizzy shirt!" I broke out indignantly at last.

"Yeah, but yours really is just a dizzy shirt. This is an emblem."

"Is that right!"

"Yeah, that *is* right."

It was right. I watched him break it out during the next weeks for certain specific triumphs—his grade of C on a history quiz, the Battle of Midway, the retirement of Mrs. Carrian, our school dietitian, or "Lucrezia," as we called her. During the regular school terms, Phineas told me, he wore the shirt principally to celebrate the victories of the soccer, hockey, and lacrosse squads. He had elected to play, and therefore inevitably to star, on these three teams the previous year. He excelled at any sport because he had never yet realized that a player had to work for years to master completely one co-ordinated athletic movement, such as swinging a golf club. He thought an athlete naturally was good at everything at once. And he was right, for himself.

But why had he picked these teams, which drew smaller crowds and commanded less prestige than some of the others? It looked a little phony to me, deliberately turning his back on fame so that people would admire him even more. That might be it. So I asked him.

"Football!" he exclaimed in a tone of thrilling scorn. "Who would ever want to play football!" We were walking across the playing fields toward the gym after an hour of compulsory calisthenics. "It's just like those damn pushups and knee bends today. 'All together now, one-two-three,' that's football. Do you know they draw a map of every player's move, like it was geometry or something?"

Privately I thought that gave football a praise-worthy orderliness. I was going to say so, but Finny had encountered one of his principles, and wanted to enlarge on it.

"In a sport you've got to be loose," he went on. "You have to invent something new all the time. It's no fun if you don't."

This, as it turned out, was his personal athletic code. To be free, to invent, to create without any imposed plan. There was the essence of happiness. Or at least, as we walked back to the gym that late afternoon, so he gave me to believe.

He applied the same individualism, or anarchy, to his studies. We were sitting in our room memorizing the Presidents of the United States one night. "Washington-Adams-Jefferson-Madison-Monroe-Adams-Jackson," said Finny. "I've got those guys cold. Then who was there?"

"Van Buren-Harrison-Tyler-Polk-Taylor-Fillmore."

"What!" Finny cried. "Who ever heard of *them!*"

"Well, they were President of the United States once."

He smiled as though at a wry, touching dream. "I guess *somebody* has to make up lists for school-boys."

I turned back to the Cleveland-Harrison-Cleveland-McKinley-Roosevelt-Taft period with a divided mind. With Phineas sitting next to me day after day like some guiltless doubting Thomas, I began to wonder not whether history was real, but whether it was important.

I didn't do well in that course; that is, I got a B. At the end of the summer Mr. Patch-Withers told me that I didn't receive an A because of a "veiled flippance" in some of my work. But by that time nothing like grades mattered any more.

I knew Finny was interfering with my studies, and then I began to suspect why. I was smarter than he was. He couldn't stand that. I wasn't deceived by that amazed, happy grin of his when he learned I'd scored the highest grade in Latin, or his candid questions about how I balanced trigonometry equations in three steps while he took twelve. He was trying to take me in; he hated the fact that I could beat him at this. He might be the best natural athlete in the school, the most popular boy, but I was winning where it counted. Of all that there was to know about Phineas, I grasped this hidden enmity best.

And then I realized, with relief, that we were equals. He wasn't so unlike me, so peacefully himself, unconscious of conflict and rivalry, after all. He was as vulnerable and treacherous as everybody else. I began to feel more comfortable with him; I almost even liked him.

Summer moved on in its measureless peace. Finny put up with the compulsory calisthenics in the afternoons, but it was in the hour or two of daylight after supper that he set out to enjoy himself. One evening when five of us were sitting around the Common Room, all bored except Phineas, the idea came to him. His face lit up in inspiration. "I know, let's go jump in the river!" The rest of us looked up warily. "You know," he said, already full of enthusiasm, "out of that tree the seniors use to practice abandoning a troopship." He looked at us in the amused, cajoling way he had, as though we were a good but reluctant team and he was the coach. "Come on, don't just sit there waiting for the end of the world."

So we went out across the empty campus. There was a heightened, theatrical glow around us, as though we were crossing an empty stage with light flooding out from the wings. It gave what we were about to do the aura of a drama.

The tree grew alone and leaned out slightly over the river's edge. We looked up at its extraordinary height, and none of us believed that we would jump from it. None but Phineas. He stripped to his underpants and began scrambling up the wooden rungs nailed on the side of the tree. At last he stepped onto a branch which reached out a little farther over the water. "Is this the one they jump from?" he called down. None of us knew. "If I do it, will everybody do it?" We didn't say anything very clearly. "Well," he cried out, "here's my contribution to the war effort!" and he sprang out, fell through the tips of some lower branches, and smashed into the water.

"Great!" he cried, bobbing instantly to the surface again. "That's the most fun I've had this whole week. Who's next?"

I was. I hated the very existence of that tree. The idea of jumping from it revolted every instinct for self-preservation I had. But I would not lose in this to Phineas. I took off my clothes and began to climb. The branch he had jumped from was more slender than it looked from the ground, and much higher. It was impossible to walk out on it far enough to be well over the river. I would have to spring far out or risk falling into the shallows next to the bank. "Come on," drawled Finny from below, "don't admire the view. When they torpedo the troopship you can't stand around admiring the waves. Jump!"

It took one hatred to overcome another. I hated him at that moment, always trying to show me up, to get revenge for my procession of A's and his of D's. Damn him. I jumped.

The tips of branches snapped past me and then I crashed into the water. An instant later I was on the surface getting congratulations.

"I think that was better than Finny's," said Bobby Zane, who was bidding for an ally in the dispute he foresaw.

"Oh, yeah?" Finny grimaced in pretended fury. "Let's see you pass the course before you start handing out grades. The tree's all yours."

Bobby's mouth closed as though forever. He didn't argue or refuse. He became inanimate. But the other two, Chet Douglass and Leper Lepellier, were vocal enough, complaining about school regulations, the danger of stomach cramps, chronic infirmities they had never mentioned before.

"It's you, pal," Finny said to me at last, "just you and me." He and I started back across the campus, preceding the others like two seigneurs.

But this made me feel no closer to Phineas. Neither did the document he drew up, the Charter of the Super Suicide Society of the Summer Session, inscribing his name and mine as charter members. He listed Chet, Bobby, and Leper as "trainees," and posted the paper in the Common Room. A few added their names to the trainee list and came with us in the evenings. The thing was respected: Finny's direct and aspiring pleasure in this game carried the whole dormitory with him.

August arrived with a deepening of all the summertime splendors of New Hampshire. There was a latent freshness in the air, as though spring were returning in the middle of the summer.

But examinations were at hand. I wasn't as ready for them as I should have been. The Suicide Society now met almost every evening, and all members were required to attend and jump. I never got inured to it. But when Phineas did it backwards one evening, so did I, with the sensation that I was throwing my life away. He promoted both of us on the spot to Senior Overseer Charter Members.

I would not let myself be shaken off, even though I began to see that it didn't really matter whether he showed me up at the tree or not. Because it was what you had in your heart that counted. And I had detected that Finny's was a den of lonely, selfish ambition. He was not better than I was, no matter who won all the contests.

A French examination was announced for one Friday late in August. Finny and I studied for it in the library Thursday afternoon; I went over vocabulary lists, and he wrote messages and passed them with great seriousness to me, as *aides-mémoire*. Of course I didn't get any work done. After supper I went to our room to try again. Phineas came in.

"Arise," he began airily, "Senior Overseer Charter Member! Elwin 'Leper' Lepellier has announced his intention to make the leap this very night, to qualify, to save his face at last."

I didn't believe it. Leper Lepellier would go down paralyzed with panic on any sinking troopship before making such a jump. Finny had put him up to it, to finish me for good on the exam. I turned around with elaborate resignation. "If he jumps out of that tree I'm Mahatma Gandhi."

"All right," Finny agreed. He had a way of turning clichés inside out like that. "Come on. We've got to be there. Maybe he *will* do it this time."

"Jee-sus!" I slammed the French book shut.

"What's the matter?"

What a performance! His face was completely questioning and candid. "Studying!" I snarled. "You know, books. Examinations."

"Yeah . . . " He waited for me to go on, as though he didn't see what I was getting at yet.

"Oh, of course, *you* wouldn't know what I'm talking about. Not you." I stood up and slammed the chair against the desk. "Okay, we go. We watch little lily-liver Lepellier not jump from the tree, and I ruin my grade."

He looked at me with an interested expression. "You want to study?"

I sighed heavily. "Never mind, forget it. I know. I joined the club. I'm going."

"Don't go!" He shrugged. "What the hell, it's only a game."

I stopped halfway to the door. "What d'you mean?" I muttered. What he meant was clear enough, but I was groping for what lay behind his words. I might have asked, "Who are you, then?" instead. I was facing a total stranger.

"I didn't know you needed to study," he said simply. "I didn't think you ever did. I thought it just came to you."

It seemed that he had made some kind of parallel between my studies and his sports. He probably thought anything you were good at came without effort. He didn't know yet that he was unique.

I couldn't quite achieve a normal speaking voice. "If I need to study, then so do you."

"Me?" He smiled faintly. "Listen, I could study forever and I'd never break C. But it's different for you, you're good. You really are. If I had a brain like that, I'd—I'd have my head cut open so people could look at it."

He put his hands on the back of a chair and leaned toward me. "I know. We kid around a lot, but you have to be serious sometime, about something. If you're really good at something, I mean if there's nobody, or hardly anybody, who's as good as you are, then you've got to be serious about that. Don't mess around." He frowned. "Why didn't you say you had to study before?"

"Wait a minute," I said.

"It's okay. I'll oversee old Leper. I know he's not going to do it." He was at the door.

"Wait a minute," I said more sharply. "I'm coming."

"No you aren't, pal, you're going to study."

"Never mind my studying."

"You think you've done enough already?"

"Yes." I let this drop curtly, to bar him from telling me what to do about my work. He let it go at that, and went out the door ahead of me, whistling off key.

We followed our gigantic shadows across the campus, and Phineas began talking in wild French, to give me a little extra practice. I said nothing, my mind exploring the new dimensions of isolation around me. Any feat I had ever had of the tree was nothing beside this. It wasn't my neck but my understanding that was menaced. He had never been jealous of me. Now I knew that there never had been and never could have been any rivalry between us. I was not of the same quality as he.

I couldn't stand this. We reached the others loitering around the base of the tree, and Phineas began exuberantly to throw off his clothes, delighted by the challenge, the competitive tension of all of us. "Let's go, you and me," he called. A new idea struck him. "We'll go together, a double jump! Neat, eh?"

None of this mattered now: I would have listlessly agreed to anything. He started up the wooden rungs and I began climbing behind, up to the limb high over the bank. Phineas ventured a little way along it, holding a thin, nearby branch for support. "Come out a little way," he said, "and then we'll jump side by side." The countryside was striking from here, a deep-green sweep of playing fields and bordering shrubbery, with the school stadium white and miniature-looking across the river. From behind us the last long rays of light cut across the campus.

Holding firmly to the trunk, I took a step toward him, and then my knees bent and I jounced the limb. Finny, his balance gone, swung his head around to look at me for an instant with extreme interest, and then he tumbled sideways, broke through the little branches below and hit the bank with a sickening, unnatural thud. It was the first clumsy physical action I had ever seen him make. With unthinking sureness I moved out on the limb and jumped into the river, every trace of my fear of this forgotten.

None of us was allowed near the infirmary during the next days, but I heard all the rumors that came out of it. Eventually a fact emerged: one of his legs had been "shattered." I learned no more, although the subject was discussed endlessly. Everyone talked about Phineas to me. I suppose this was natural. I had been right beside him when it happened: I was his roommate.

I couldn't go on hearing about it much longer. If anyone had been suspicious of me, I might have developed some strength to defend myself. But no one suspected. Phineas must still be too sick, or too noble, to tell them.

I spent as much time as I could alone in our room, trying to empty my mind of every thought, to forget where I was, even who I was. One evening when I was dressing for dinner an idea occurred to me, the first with any energy behind it since Finny fell from the tree. I decided to put on his clothes. We wore the same size, and although he always criticized my clothes, he used to wear them frequently, quickly forgetting what belonged to him and what to me. I never forgot, and that evening I put on his cordovan shoes and his pants, and I looked for and finally found his pink shirt neatly folded, in a drawer. Its high stiff collar against my neck, the rich material against my skin excited a sense of strangeness and distinction; I felt like some nobleman, some Spanish grandee.

But when I looked in the mirror it was no remote aristocrat I had become. I was Phineas, Phineas to the life. I even had his humorous expression on my face, his sharp awareness. I had no idea why this gave me such intense relief, but it seemed, as I stood there in Finny's shirt, that I would never stumble over the twists and pitfalls of my own character again.

I didn't go down to dinner. The sense of transformation stayed with me throughout the evening, and even when I undressed and went to bed. That night I slept easily, and it was only on waking up that this illusion was gone, and I was confronted with myself, and what I had done to Finny.

Sooner or later it had to happen, and that morning it did. "Finny's better!" Dr. Stanpole called to me on the chapel steps. He steered me amiably into the lane leading toward the infirmary. "He could stand a visitor or two now, after these very nasty few days."

"You—you don't think I'll upset him or anything?"

"You? No, why? It'll do him good."

"I suppose he's still pretty sick."

"It was a messy break, but we'll have him walking again."

"*Walking* again!"

"Yes." The doctor didn't look at me, and barely changed his tone of voice. "Sports are finished for him after an accident like that, of course."

"But he must be able to," I burst out, "if his leg's still there, if you aren't going to amputate it—you aren't, are you?—then it must come back the way it was, why shouldn't it? Of course it will."

Dr. Stanpole hesitated, and I think glanced at me for a moment. "Sports are finished. As a friend you ought to help him face that and accept it."

I grabbed my head and the doctor, trying to be kind, put his hand on my shoulder. At his touch I lost all hope of controlling myself. I burst out crying into my hands; I cried for Phineas and for myself and for this doctor who believed in facing things. Most of all I cried because of kindness, which I had not expected.

"Now, that's no good. You've got to be cheerful and hopeful. He needs that from you. He wanted especially to see you. You were the one person he asked for."

That stopped my tears. Of course I was the first person he wanted to see. Phineas would say nothing behind my back; he would accuse me, face to face.

We were walking up the steps of the infirmary. Everything was very swift, and next I was in a corridor, being nudged by Dr. Stanpole toward a door. "He's in there. I'll be with you in a minute."

I pushed back the door, which was slightly ajar, and stood transfixed on the threshold. Phineas lay among pillows and sheets, his left leg, enormous in its white bindings, suspended a little above the bed. A tube led from a glass bottle into his right arm.

Some channel began to close inside me and I knew I was about to black out.

"Come on in," he said. "You look worse than I do." The fact that he could make a light remark pulled me back a little, and I went to a chair beside his bed. He seemed to have diminished physically in the few days which had passed, and to have lost his tan. His eyes studied me as though I were the patient. They no longer had their sharp good humor, but had become clouded and visionary. After a while I realized he had been given a drug. "What are *you* looking so sick about?" he went on.

"Finny, I—" there was no controlling what I said; the words were instinctive, like the reactions of someone cornered. "What happened at the tree? That damn tree, I'm going to cut down that tree. Who cares who can jump out of it? How did you fall, how could you fall off like that?"

"I just fell." His eyes looked vaguely into my face. "Something jiggled and I fell over. I remember I turned around and looked at you; it was like I had all the time in the world. I thought I could reach out and get hold of you."

I flinched violently away from him. "To drag me down too!"

He kept looking vaguely over my face. "To get hold of you, so I wouldn't fall."

"Yes, naturally." I was fighting for air in this close room. "I tried, you remember? I reached out but you were gone, down through those little branches."

"I remember looking at your face for a second. Funny expression you had. Very shocked, like you have right now."

"Right now? Well, of course, I *am* shocked. It's terrible."

"But I don't see why you should look so *personally* shocked. You look like it happened to you or something."

"It's almost like it did! I was right there, right on the limb beside you!"

"Yes, I know. I remember it all."

There was a hard block of silence, and then I said quietly, as though my words might detonate the room, "Do you remember what made you fall?"

His eyes continued their roaming across my face. "I don't know. I must have lost my balance. It must have been that. I did have this feeling that when you were standing there beside me, y—I don't know. I must have been delirious. So I just have to forget it. I just fell, that's all." He turned away to grope for something among the pillows. "I'm sorry about that feeling I had."

I couldn't say anything to this sincere, drugged apology for having suspected the truth. He was never going to accuse me. It was only a feeling he had, and at this moment he must have been formulating a new commandment in his personal decalogue: Never accuse a friend of a crime if you only have a feeling he did it.

It was his best victory. If I had been the one in the hospital bed I would have brought Devon down around his ears with my accusations; I would have hounded him out of the school. And I had thought we were competitors! It was so ludicrous I wanted to cry.

And if Phineas had been sitting here in this pool of guilt, how would he have felt, what would he have done?

He would have told the truth.

I got up so suddenly that the chair overturned. I stared at him in amazement, and he stared back, his mouth gradually breaking into a grin. "Well," he said in his friendly, knowing voice, "what are you going to do, hypnotize me?"

"Finny, I've got something to tell you. You're going to hate it, but there's something I've got to tell you."

But I didn't tell him. Dr. Stanpole came in before I was able to, and then a nurse came in, and I was sent away. I walked down the corridor of elms descending from the infirmary to the dormitories, and at every tree I seemed to leave something I had envied Finny—his popularity, his skill at sports, his background, his ease. It was none of these I had wanted from him. It was the honesty of his every move and his every thought.

But the story wasn't yet complete. I had to wait for a while before ending it, because the day after I saw Finny, the doctor decided that he was not yet well enough for visitors, even old pals like me, after all. The summer session closed. Phineas was taken by ambulance to his home outside Boston, and I went south for a month's vacation. At the end of September I came back to Boston, en route to Devon for the fall term. I found the town where he lived, and I waited a little longer under that tree in front of Finny's house, struggling, maybe for the last time, with the risky emotions I had had for years. Tomorrow, back at Devon, I would be someone else. A week later I was going to turn seventeen and begin the last acceleration which would pitch me into some corner of the war.

The sun was going down much earlier those days,

and it began to get chilly. I rehearsed what I was going to say once more, and then turned in through the hedge and knocked at Finny's door.

The
Reading
of the Will

T here was no reading of the will at all. Three days after Ernest Curtin's unforeshadowed death from a heart attack, his son Christopher opened the safe-deposit box and found it, wedged between some A. T. & T. certificates, ridges of U. S. Steel, a pile of Du Pont, government bonds. The estate was in a very viable condition. There were also some old school report cards, some out-of-date family jewelry, lists of holdings, financial footnotes.

Christopher pulled the will out from this welter and unfolded it. There were two witnesses with him, a Mr. Williams of the bank's trust department, who was to be one of the executors of the estate, and Christopher's uncle, George Curtin, the other.

He began swiftly scanning it: " . . . to my beloved wife . . . bequeath . . . irrevocable trust . . . my sole legatee . . . she shall have in addition . . . trust . . . furthermore . . . all monies . . . "

"Give it to him," said George Curtin, indicating Mr. Williams.

Christopher went on quickly scanning the document, which, in view of the shoals of assets that had surrounded it, was surprisingly short; as nearly as he could make out from the swiftness of his reading and the legalisms of the writing, absolutely everything had been left to his mother.

"Give it to Mr. Williams," his uncle repeated a shade more impatiently.

Christopher stared at the will for a moment or two and then took a sidelong look at his uncle. "Do you mind if I read my father's will?" he asked evenly.

"You should already know the gist," George Curtin answered with a shrug.

"I'm interested in the wording," Christopher said through set teeth.

The two other men proceeded to spread out the securities on top of the oval mahogany table in this private conference room provided by the First National Bank of Connecticut at Hartford for certain major transactions of its major accounts.

All the stock certificates crackled wealthily as they were unfolded and sorted. None of them was in the name of either Christopher or his older brother, Ernest, Jr.; all were either part of their father's estate or already owned by their mother. There were a few flukes, defaulted highway bonds, expropriated foreign companies, but most were as solid as anything could be. Ernest Curtin's idea of taking a flier had been to buy into the Columbia Broadcasting System or Trans World Airlines.

"I'm hungry," said Christopher suddenly.

"Shall I send out for something?" suggested Mr. Williams. "Unless you would like to go out for lunch and go on later . . . "

"Let's go on," said George Curtin. "I'd like a sandwich and coffee, though."

Food was ordered and by the time it arrived, the tangible results of Ernest Curtin's much-admired and envied life were arranged in seven rather small piles on the shining solid-mahogany tabletop. He had, really, devoted his life to this moment: that these seven piles of paper would be lying here on this table.

There was one very singular remaining item. It was a large manila envelope addressed to Ernie, who was far away, sick with hepatitis in Cairo, where he worked as Middle East correspondent for *World Geography* magazine and also, his brother sometimes suspected, as a spy. He presumed that if that was true, he was a spy for the United States; but Ernie being Ernie, he couldn't be certain.

In this conventional, orderly, deeply conservative group of documents, the envelope was as conspicuous as a red flag. What could it mean, with its nervously scrawled inscription, its urgency, its secretiveness? The three men spent a great deal of time dealing with the other papers, shuffling them and rearranging them, drawing up lists of them, checking and rechecking what they were already perfectly sure of: that the estate was in immaculate order.

At last they turned their attention to the manila envelope.

"Addressed to Ernest," said George Curtin.

"Yes."

"Of course, your father never imagined Ernest wouldn't be here at a time like this."

"No, he couldn't have foreseen that."

"As a matter of face, he did," Mr. Williams put in. He indicated the words written by the deceased beneath the large scrawled "To My Son Ernest Curtin, Jr.—Strictly Private and Strictly Personal—To Be Opened Privately Only By Him." Underneath, in an only somewhat less emphatic script, was written, "In the event he predeceases me, the envelope is to be immediately burned. This is my express final wish, which I solemnly instruct be honored by my heirs and executors." And beneath that, written in all its familiar, hurried forcefulness, was the signature.

"But, of course," said Christopher irritably, "that isn't foreseeing the present situation at all."

"No, not this specific situation," murmured Mr. Williams.

George Curtin had picked up the envelope and was holding it before him, turning it slowly back and forth. "If he doesn't come for the funeral, we'll send it to him, special delivery and registered, and so on."

"To Egypt?" said Christopher.

George Curtin just looked at his nephew in his formidable, ex-football-lineman-with-brains way.

"You can't send anything as confidential as that through the mails to Egypt," Christopher went on.

The fixed irritation of George Curtin's face reminded Christopher very much of the way his brother had contemplated him from time to time. Finally, the uncle said flatly, "Why not?"

Always better informed than anyone else in his family, Christopher had learned some years before to underplay this advantage, if that was what it was. In a great many respects, it had seemed to him a drawback. "Egypt's a military dictatorship," he murmured hurriedly. "Everything's censored. Who knows what's in there? We might not want it read."

To cover his ignorance about Egypt, George Curtin attacked on the other point, Christopher noticed without surprise. "What could be in there that's so bloody special, such a secret?"

Christopher chuckled. "Maybe Ernie and I are adopted."

George Curtin put the envelope down on the table. "Do you have any objection to sending even that information to Egypt? Some wog finds out you're adopted, so what? I was at the hospital the day you were born and I was there the day Ernie was born, and so I sort of don't think that's probably what's in there."

Christopher took a one-beat pause, which he knew would infuriate his uncle, having gotten tired of his policy of appeasement, and then said, "It's too risky. Ernie's got his job and his family and everything in Egypt. They throw foreigners out all the time, on any pretext. They expropriate their property. Who knows what's in there? It could be anything. It's too risky. We could get Ernie into a tremendous amount of trouble."

There was a silence and the George Curtin muttered, "It's just something about 'Take care of your mother.' "

After another, longer silence, Mr. Williams said encouragingly, "These highway bonds here . . . " and uncle and nephew turned resolutely to examine the highway bonds.

The funeral had been postponed two days, in the hope that Ernest, Jr., would be well enough to fly home.

It was three in the afternoon when Christopher got home. The house, capacious Colonial Connecticut in design, was choked by banks and mounds and cascades of flowers, so intolerably odorous that their fumes transformed the atmosphere of this respectable family place into that of, it seemed to him, some Oriental love garden, some Persian terrace, corrupt and drugging. It was as inappropriate and as sickening as possible. His father's body, which he instinctively and absolutely would not approach, certain that he would find not his father, not the body of his father but some cosmetician's violation, was in the living room. The house was also full of excruciatingly helpful friends. "He looks more rested today," one lady said to him. Stricken, Christopher could only stare at her. Then someone came up out of the hubbub to say that there was an overseas telephone call. He went into the library and locked the door. It was Ernie calling from the hospital in Cairo, his voice coming through very faintly, squeezed by being transmitted five thousand miles, the volume rising and fading, as tenuous, Christopher suddenly reflected, as tenuous as life.

" . . . there," he heard his brother yelling. "I need to be!"

"Are you coming?" he yelled back.

"I can't come. The doctor here absolutely says no. I feel ugrah—"

"What?"

Barbara's voice came threading to him across the world. "He's too ill to travel. He just can't. He just can't."

Then Ernie's voice again: "How's Mother?"

"She's going to be all right." Then he heard himself blurt, "Dad left everything to her."

"What?"

"She inherited everything."

"I can't hear you."

"You will."

"For Christ's sake, can't you speak louder? I'm in Egypt!"

"MOTHER GOT EVERYTHING."

Silence ensued in Egypt. Then he heard Ernie say, his voice as thin as a needle, "I hope you . . . taking . . . arrangements."

"There's a special letter for you from Dad. How shall we get it to you, now that we know you can't come? I was afraid you couldn't."

"What's in the letter?"

"It's confidential to you. I don't know what's in it."

"I hope you know what you're doing about everything. I hate . . . so sick."

"Take it easy. Everything's all right. Get better soon. I'm going to get Mother now to talk to you."

"I hope you know what you're doing about everything there."

"Get better soon. Good-bye."

The funeral took place two days later in the Congregational Church. It was well attended, for a funeral, and it helped a little. The fact that funerals happened so often, that there was an age-old formula of words and a prescribed service, immemorially performed and reperformed, helped a little.

But then came the snow-sopped cemetery, the casket, the flowers, the tent, fake grass, minister, handful of mourners. It was intolerable that this was happening at all; and at the same time, it should not be happening so fast. It was indecent, disrespectful, brutal; it was a violation.

As the family was leaving the side of the grave through the slush, Christopher was overcome with a sudden fear: "They are not going to bury my father. Once we are gone, they will take the body and sell it to some medical school or just throw it away." He would certainly have stayed and seen that the interment—he flinched as this word crossed his mind in reference to the human being who had been his father—that the interment was carried out to the last detail, except for the thought that if they were really resolute body snatchers, he could stand there guarding it, and when he was gone, they could dig his father up and dispose of him any way they wanted. It was all intolerable.

"I can't believe he isn't going to say anything else

to me," Christopher blurted to his mother and uncle in the car driving away. "I just can't believe it. I *don't* believe it. It isn't possible."

"Well . . . "

"I . . . all those conversations and phone calls and letters and advice and arguments and orders and fights and all that, ever since I was born. It isn't *over* yet. He hadn't finished what he started to say. He's been *interrupted*. He's been interrupted."

Following lunch—roast lamb and boiled potatoes —the Heiress and the Prodigal Son, as Christopher now pictured them, since his mother had been left all the property and his brother had been left the only message and he himself had simply been left, quitted, the Heiress and the Prodigal Son sat down with Uncle George around the large oval table in the library to contemplate the manila envelope addressed to Ernest.

At first George suggested they mail it, but then Christopher's point about censorship was acknowledged. George thought of a friend in the State Department who might put it in the diplomatic pouch to Cairo, but that was discarded as impractical and possibly illegal. Mrs. Curtin suggested waiting until Ernie's next planned return to America but was reminded that that was nearly a year away. They finally concluded that the manila envelope would have to be taken by hand to him in Cairo. No one knew anyone planning such a trip. Someone would have to go expressly for this purpose. Who? There was no more appropriate person than Christopher— not married, twenty-three, just out of college and just about to be drafted.

"I'll go," he said, "but not by plane."

"Not a plane?" said Uncle George. "It would take weeks by ship. Of course you'll fly. Why not?"

"I'll go. But not by plane."

He was afraid he might be killed if he flew. Sudden death had suddenly become terribly possible. Before, it was something that had happened to others, other people, other families. With horror, he had seen the people on the sidewalks look with certain interest at the hearse carrying a member of *his* family and at the black limousine carrying him move slowly along toward the cemetery, just as he had looked with mild interest often at the funerals of strangers. But now it was his own father, his family, and he was a mourner, which he had never had any intention of being. Sudden death: it existed.

"I'll go. But I won't take a plane."

He sailed from New York first class on the *Cristoforo Colombo* on January 10. The manila envelope, with its urgent, scrawled directions, traveled with him like an unexamined bomb.

To take his mind off it and off death itself, he tried to read, settling into a deck chair on the enclosed promenade deck. All of the other chairs were occupied by married couples in their fifties and sixties and seventies, for this was just the sort of winter trip to a mild climate that attracted them. The men wore expensive tweeds and sweaters or sports jackets, the women wore carefully harmonized skirts, blouses and sweaters that buttoned up the front, and they all looked affluent, comfortable and rather optimistic. In just these kinds of clothes, in just this kind of style, with just such expressions on their faces, Mr. and Mrs. Ernest Curtin sailed from New York to Venezuela, had sailed through the Canal to California and Hawaii, had sailed to Lapland and the Baltic Sea, had circled the Mediterranean, visited the Greater and Lesser Antilles, had sailed around the world.

Every day after lunch all of the elderly couples, and Christopher, would gather up a book or some stationery and repair to their deck chairs, spread blankets over their knees, contemplate the empty Atlantic becoming every day a little more benign as they proceeded toward Gibraltar, and every day, sooner or later, most of the older people would fall gently asleep.

Seeing this was by far the worst experience he had had since the sight of his father's casket about to be lowered (or not lowered!) into the wintry ground. The old people became effigies on their own future coffins when they fell asleep, heads back, mouths slightly open, color growing waxen, postures final, ultimate, hands folded on the lap or crossed like Egyptian mummies on the chest, they lay there in these long reclining chairs very clearly, to his hypersleepless stare, rehearsing, every day after lunch, for the coming arrangement of their bodies in the horror of the plush inner lining of their caskets.

Then an old lady would stir, the eyes reluctantly open, blank at this return from the edge, re-collect herself gradually, glance at the old male body lying motionless beside her, and her slowly returning animation would communicate itself to him, he would stir, shake slightly, pull himself once more, this time, back into the living world and, two Lazaruses, they would say to each other, "Shall we have some tea?" and "I dropped off there for a little while," "So did I, I think," and then, slowly, they would rise.

But the people and the reading and the ship and the Atlantic Ocean itself could not keep his mind off the manila envelope. He was beginning to think he ought to ... to *do* something about it. It lay at the bottom of the smaller of his two suitcases, under his accumulating dirty laundry, where he also concealed his traveler's checks and his passport. He extricated the envelope from this hiding place before dinner the third day out from New York and turned it in his hands this way and that. The envelope was quite opaque, no matter how strong the light he held it in front of. It felt rather thick, as though there were a number of sheets of paper—or, for example, stock certificates—inside, or something like a birth certificate ("Your brother was adopted from a fisherman and his common-law wife in Provincetown ... ") or medical documents ("Following my examination of Christopher Curtin, age four, I hereby certify that he is suffering from hereditary, congenital and incurable ... ") or legal documents ("In this confidential codicil to my last will and testament, I, Ernest Curtin, Senior, do order and direct that my younger son, Christopher, be disinherited upon the demise of myself and my wife, unless he will agree to enter the ministry of the Congregational Church ... ").

Ridiculous fantasies, although in the Curtin family, nothing was ever *really* impossible; and also, what could his mind do but invent such things when it didn't *know?* There might be something truly precious within the manila envelope, perhaps a confidential diary his father had kept, a record of his inner life and profoundest thoughts, of his hopes for the family's future that he wanted to communicate to his older son and only to his older son. Or was he passing on to Ernie some task, some duty, that he, and only he, the older, was to be allowed to perform for their father? Why were the survivors ordered to destroy it unopened if Ernie had died first? What could he and only he be allowed to see?

He began to wonder if there might be a jet of steam somewhere on board, around the ship swimming pool, maybe, or in the kitchens. And then he immediately put that thought out of his mind.

It was of very stiff, firm manila paper, the flap sealed in the ordinary way with glue.

The *Ausonia,* the ship he'd boarded at Naples, docked at Alexandria in the afternoon on January 20. The wild uproar on the dock, vendors and porters and taximen yelling and scrambling, established the theme of the remainder of the day and maybe, he thought of his stay in Egypt and even of his whole future life.

For it was now to be a Life Without Father, and who knew into what confusion, even chaos, that might lead him, especially when his mother was so vague and impractical and his brother lived on the other side of the world and didn't always particularly like him?

A gaggle of porters in dirty white-and-blue striped pajamas with rags on their heads swept up to him, yelling and gesticulating, and he was immediately engulfed in Egypt. Eventually he found himself in the customs shed, and the official asked him to open the smaller of his two suitcases. As he opened the bag its contents divided into halves, and the manila envelope, which he had buried in his dirty laundry in the middle, came face up on top. Both he and the inspector gazed down at it.

"Personal material?" inquired the inspector.

"Yes, it is—"

"This is your name? It is not, is it?"

"That's my brother. He is a"—*spy* almost sprang out of his rattled mind—"a correspondent, *World*

Geography magazine, in Cairo. This is just—I'm taking it to him . . . "

The inspector fished around the contents of the bag briefly, and then it was over and he was admitted to the country and obtained some Egyptian pounds and piasters, tattered and smelling of camel and horse and sweat and poverty and desperation; and with these scattered like confetti on all sides, he got himself and his two suitcases out of the shed, into the bright warm afternoon sunshine, into a corrupt taxi with a gangster at the wheel, through a ramshackle, teeming Alexandria, alive with children everywhere, to the railroad station, cursing himself regularly for his sudden phobia against flying, got his ticket with delays and difficulties, waited a long time before being able to board the train, waited another long time before the train started, and then it proceeded at a very cautious rate of speed up the delta of the Nile to Cairo, where he arrived at precisely the time he had not wanted to arrive, dead of night. Not only that, but he had gotten reservations at a hotel that was well out of town, out in the Sahara apparently, a hotel that he had chosen because it "overlooked the Great Pyramid"; and in America, that had seemed very important.

Christopher seemed to be almost the only traveler, and certainly the only foreigner, in the vast and hollow nighttime station, as he made his way through it, his bags being carried by an old man in a gray dress, whose eyes were very badly crossed.

On the street the porter began installing his bags in a taxi and Christopher was struck by the look of its driver, an assassin with pointed teeth, black hair standing on end, and the blazing grin of a maniac. Spread over his knees and tied by a string to the steering column was a dark-brown hawk whose wings, spread, would have measured approximately four feet.

His bags were already in this taxi and there was, in fact, no other waiting, so he slowly gave the porter money, got into the back, which had linoleum on the floor and plastic-covered seats, and, its motor rattling uncertainly, the taxi set off into the blackness.

The hawk now moved to the seat beside the driver and began to open its wings, fixing one eye on the passenger in the back seat. They were passing an intersection with a streetlight on the corner, and the driver grabbed the bird and shoved it onto the floor so it would not be seen. Christopher thought one of its wings was broken by this treatment, but when they were on a dark stretch of road again, the bird climbed back onto the seat and partially spread its wings again.

"English?" said the driver, grinning back at him.

"American."

"Ah."

They were driving along a broad road lined with large trees and they kept driving on and on and on. There were almost no people and no cars anywhere. The driver continued to manhandle the hawk from time to time. The hawk had not retaliated yet. Then the driver pulled over to the side of the road, said something unintelligible, got out, disappeared, returned, got back in, and drove on. A number of possibilities as to what he had done, all unpleasant, occurred to Christopher.

"You have American money?" he asked suddenly. "Traveler's checks?"

"Yes."

"I change. Much better than at bank. How much you have?"

"Uh—no. No. Tomorrow."

"Tomorrow?"

"Tomorrow."

They drove on.

"What are you looking for?" said the driver.

"I'm looking for the hotel overlooking the Great Pyramid. Is it near here?"

"Near. Near."

And, in fact, it was. A dimly lit driveway materialized on the right and they drove into it and stopped on the gravel before a flight of steps.

A man opened the door of the taxi. There was no one else visible and very few lights. The taxi driver asked for double what the meter showed. Christopher, feeling in a somewhat stronger position now, declined. He did give him a large tip. The hawk watched it all. So did the man who had opened the door. He went into an enormously high and silent lobby, dimly lighted. There was one man in a dark suit there asleep in an armchair. The doorman woke him up and this man registered Christopher. The silence of the building sounded unbreakable. An old man in a long white robe and a fez took him and his bags into a small elevator; it slowly rose three floors, where they got off and proceeded along a lengthy and enormous hallway, scarcely illuminated at all, arriving at last before a large door; they went into a very large pale-yellow room, with one large window at the far end, shuttered, two beds, a huge wardrobe, and very chilly air. The light was one naked bulb hanging from the ceiling.

Christopher gave the man something and then he was alone. He had a very strong feeling that he was the only guest in this huge hotel and he recalled that he was in the Sahara desert, or the Libyan Desert, or the Western Desert; in any case, he was alone in the desert. He began to unpack and had nearly finished before the lights all went out.

Instinct in this situation was very definite as to what to do. He felt his way to the bed, took off his pants and shoes, pulled back the covers, got into bed and pulled the covers over himself. Then he didn't move.

Some kind of yelling and general commotion came into the room and Christopher opened his eyes—he had, after all, been asleep—and saw that daylight had also come into the room through the shutters and banished the specters of the night before. He got out of bed, threw back the huge shutters, and there, without any doubt at all, was the Great Pyramid of Giza; the hotel did not, of course, overlook it; it overlooked the hotel, on a rise a few hundred yards away, gray, the essence of massiveness and of triangularity. All sorts of camels and horses and carriages and hundreds of people surged between the hotel and the pyramid.

Everything was as animated this morning as it had been sepulchral the night before. It was possible that the telephone in the room, which he had not even bothered to pick up, so dead had it looked, worked. He picked it up, a human voice responded, and he gave the number of his brother's house in Maadi, a suburb of Cairo. Barbara answered.

"You're here at last," she said. "We were so surprised when Mother Curtin wrote that you were coming by *boat*. How funny, we thought."

Christopher, instantly put off, said, "I'll tell you all about it. How's Ernie?"

"Still very weak. It's an absolutely filthy disease. I had no idea. Of course, it's from plain malnutrition.

We just can't get the right food in this country. Do you like Mena House?"

After a pause he answered, "More and more."

"I wish we could have had you here, but with the baby—"

"I'm fine here. When shall I see you and Ernie?"

"He wants us to come at six o'clock. Shall I pick you up there at five-thirty? What will you do all day? If it wasn't for the baby and my committee meeting, I could take you around. I hope you've got something to do today."

"Of course I do. First I'm going to go over to that big stone thing that comes to a point across the road and do whatever you do to it. Do you climb it or do you go into it?"

"I don't think they climb it any more," she said.

It was true that people were no longer allowed to climb it. "Too many slip" the ancient robed guide explained, "And when they start to fall on the Great Pyramid, they never stop—*bang-bang-bang-bang,* like down a staircase, all the way to the bottom."

But a visitor could go into it, up the outer face on steps cut into one of the immense gray stone blocks, then into a tunnel winding toward the depths, arriving finally at the strangest chamber on earth, called the Grand Gallery, rather narrow, extremely high, the haunting gray walls sloping toward each other as they rose, lighted by electricity, the floor rising very steeply upward and farther upward, the bottom end of the gallery blocked by a stone too immense to be thought about, and its upper end giving onto a large empty chamber with purple granite walls.

It was only on arriving at last in this core of the unbelievable mass, having only half listened to the guide, that Christopher realized, or recollected, that the Great Pyramid was a tomb, was in fact the very apex of death, that he was standing in the Pharaoh's burial chamber, and that the unthinkable human effort which went into erecting this had been that man's effort to defeat death, to carry himself beyond it.

But the chamber was completely empty; it had been robbed of everything thousands of years before.

Barbara was her usual extremely prompt self. How she managed to be that in Egypt was a riddle that Christopher, after he came to know the habits of the country better, never solved.

At five-thirty, her black Ford, with a chauffeur at the wheel, drew up at the steps of the Mena House. The robed servants, the big comfortable veranda, the Europeans having tea, Barbara with her Egyptian chauffeur, all created a small, illusory tableau of the old British Colonial days, and Barbara sustained it with her white gloves, white linen suit, dark glasses, and large hat.

They made a pass at kissing each other, then got into the back seat of the immaculately kept Ford. Barbara said, "We've got miles and miles and miles to go. The hospital's on the other side of town entirely."

They drove back along the road he had traveled the night before, and all the night before's sinister atmosphere had evaporated in the happy sunshine of what would be in Connecticut an especially fine day in late September. Apartment houses, trees, a big park, fountains all swept by; they crossed the Nile, as mighty as it should be, on through the center of Cairo, and arrived at last at a pleasant-looking U-shaped building of tan concrete, with balconies looking out over an agreeable square: Dar al Chifa Hospital.

Inside, it was very tidy and it was also very cheerful, almost festive. Nuns and imams scurried about, Bedouins and Europeans crisscrossed the lobby. "Well, this isn't so bad," he remarked.

They went up to the third floor, through a tiny vestibule banked with flowers, and into a pleasant hospital room, with French doors opening onto a balcony and the square below. Ernie was in bed, looking very ill.

He shook hands weakly, blinked up from his pillow, his redhead's light complexion paler than ever, hazel eyes a little groggy. Christopher was shocked and tried to hide it. But, of course, Ernie had to be seriously, even desperately ill not to have come back for the funeral.

Ernie had always been generally regarded as "crazy"; that is, overactive, unpredictable, hypercritical, uncontrollably impulsive, dangerous when drunk, extremely willful, and very intelligent. He had had many vicissitudes in his stormy life, and the fact that he had at last seemed to settle down, even if in Cairo, had been a great relief to everybody. The slightly askew look he had about the eyes warned some people about his nature on sight. But the basis of all the quirks of his character was his formidable, ceaseless energy. And now he didn't have any. Christopher was shocked to see this pale rag and appalled to see it after the last sight he had had of his father, lying in the way that he had been lying. My family, Christopher thought, how frail we are.

Ernie seemed to want to talk and to have enough energy for that. After describing at length the grimly depressing effects of hepatitis, he finished by murmuring, "It just makes you hope you do die."

Christopher snapped forward in his chair. "Don't say that!"

Ernie's cloudy eyes roamed over him. "Anyway, it *is* the dreariest disease in the annals of medicine. I have to say I never felt worse in my life—"

"Ernie," Barbara put in irritably, "just keeping on saying that makes it even truer."

He pulled the sides of his mouth down as he looked over at her and then went on, "And it had to happen to me at the biggest crisis we have had in the family and I had to be in Cairo, United Arab Republic. And Father, whom I loved and will always deeply miss, had to leave every red cent to Mother, every last single share of every last blue-chip stock. I'm sorry to say that. If I didn't feel so awful, I probably wouldn't say it, probably wouldn't even think it particularly, if I didn't feel so awful." He raised his head slightly. "Oh. Where's the envelope?"

Christopher started, stared at him and finally compelled himself to mumble, "I forgot it." He had never felt like such a complete fool.

Ernie forced his head a little higher. "You *forgot it!*" he said in an invalid's roar. "How could you *forget* it! That's what you came five thousand miles to give me!"

"I didn't forget it in America," Christopher rasped. "I forgot it at the hotel. Take it easy. I'll bring it tomorrow." Ernie was sinking very slowly back toward the pillow. "What's the big fuss about? After all, there's nothing so important in there." He glanced over Ernie's head. "Is there?" he murmured.

Ernie contemplated him. Finally, his right hand slid out from under the sheet and he pointed at Christopher. "I can't see visitors until six o'clock. I want it here at six o'clock tomorrow night."

Christopher leaned back in his chair and threw up his hands. "All *right!*"

That night in his huge old room in the hotel, he took out the envelope for the last time. It had never looked so potent with information or insight or instructions or wisdom, so potentially enriching, so helpful, revealing, absorbing—well, so alive.

He was certain he knew how to open it and seal it again so that Ernie wouldn't notice. What's more, if he did notice, Christopher could just say that that was how the envelope had been when he found it in the safe-deposit box, and no one could refute him. Neither Uncle George nor Mr. Williams had examined it minutely. No one in the world would ever know.

But Ernie would probably let him see its contents, anyway.

And, worst of all, there were the words in his father's handwriting, as explicit and forbidding as they could be. There were those words, in his handwriting.

But *why* had he left this message only to Ernie and not to him? Even if Ernie were dead, it was not to pass on to Christopher but had to be burned. Why? What did he lack, why couldn't he be trusted, what was the *matter* with him?

His hand trembling a little, feeling cold, very cold in this unheated night room on the edge of the great desert, Christopher held the envelope for a long time. Finally he put it on the table beside his bed and began to undress.

The next day he did the second thing after the Great Pyramid that he had been told was a necessity for a visitor, and went through the Cairo Museum.

Overwhelming statues of the Pharaohs and the gods, immense sarcophagi, the great funeral furniture of King Tutankhamen, the touching grace of the solar boat that was to carry a dead Pharaoh to his new life as a god of the sun; the mummies, swathed in brown linen, which had been peeled away on certain corpses to reveal hands or feet or a face, while others had been left completely wrapped, their little royal bodies clearly palpable beneath, recognizable still. The glory of ancient Egypt lay everywhere, their colossal attempt to sail past death itself, the huge effort they made to reach immortality, to reach the sun.

Instead, what they reached was the Cairo Museum.

Christopher left toward dusk and hailed a taxi in the great square in front of the museum to take him to the hospital. He had the manila envelope in his hand, had carried it around with him all day, his heart beating when he looked at it.

The taxi stopped for a traffic light, and across the intersection there was a group of men standing in the street, conferring. A light-brown mound was near the curb about five yards from them and it was somehow clear that the conference was related to it; it was somehow equally clear that they did not want to be too near it. The light changed; and as the taxi passed close to the mound, Christopher saw that the cloth was very similar to that which bound the mummies in the museum. There was a breeze blowing and stones had been put at the corners of the cloth to hold it down. Then he realized that there was a body under it.

"My God," he murmured.

"Traffic accident," said the driver, very calmly.

His attitude seemed callous to Christopher then, but later on he found that traffic fatalities were so everyday, the Egyptian masses having never succeeded in adapting themselves to the automobile, that he understood it better.

"Lovemaking and death," his brother would tell him a few weeks later. (The animosity between them had ended by the time Ernie said this and he was beginning to try to be helpful to Christopher, to be an adviser, a guide, for the first time. "That's all Egypt is, lovemaking and death.")

At Dar al Chifa Hospital, Christopher paid the driver and went in through the lobby, which seemed gayer than ever, people laughing and gossiping everywhere.

He reached his brother's room. Ernie looked much better today, sitting up in bed reading a newspaper. Barbara hadn't arrived yet.

"Hi," said Ernie easily, holding out his hand for the manila envelope.

With some deliberation in his manner, Christopher handed it to him. Ernie read through carefully what their father had written on the front and then turned the envelope over and proceeded to examine the flap even more carefully.

Christopher was thrown into a paroxysm of rage, thinking, That bastard, suspecting me of disobeying Father's last wish! and then controlling himself outwardly because his one hope was that Ernie, voluntarily, would let him read the contents.

"I think I'll look at this now. Might be, just might be something pressing in there. And, uh," he went on in a sincere tone, "you did take your time delivering it."

Christopher managed to control himself again.

"Why not sit out on the balcony," Ernie said, "and watch the sunset? It's one of the great sights of Egypt."

Christopher smiled agreeably, he hoped, and went out and sat on the balcony, facing a tremendous Nile sunset, depths of color and desert clarity and southern glow. Now and then he heard the hiss and crackle of sheets of paper being unfolded, shifted, arranged. He sat immobile, staring at the great sunset; he was, of course, much farther from home than he had ever been, much more of an alien than he had ever been, and now perhaps he was learning that he was an alien in his own family.

"Come on back in," Ernie called cheerfully at last, and Christopher re-entered the room to find the envelope on the night table beside the bed, face down, its flap open, its contents back inside it. Barbara had quietly arrived and was sitting in the corner. "There's a bottle of Scotch in the cupboard," Ernie went on, "if you want a drink. Not that I can have any. I'm a teetotaler—*me!*—for the next ten years or something, after hepatitis," and he sighed deeply. Ernie had, it was true, had a lot of bad breaks in his life. "Barbara, you know where the ice is down the hall. Of course, I could ring for service," he said ironically, his eyes widening into their famous incredulity glare. No more needed to be said about the service in Dar al Chifa Hospital. Barbara went out to get the ice.

Ernie began to recount his theories as to why he felt so much better today, then went on to a general account of their life in Egypt, and then asked Christopher in detail what he had seen in the museum, and never once made any reference to the envelope.

Finally and quietly and fatalistically, Christopher asked, "What was in the envelope, Ernie?"

Ernie's slightly askew eyes looked at him, the corners of his mouth went down and then he said gravely, "I just can't tell you." He drew a serious breath. "It's something Dad had to say. It's not something you need to know. Forget about it. I'll handle it."

At those last words, Christopher cursed himself for having ever imagined the mere possibility that Ernie would let him know their father's message. Ernie had always been extremely jealous of his position as older brother. "I'm four years, seven months and two days older than he is" had practically been a litany of Ernie's always. "I'll drive" had been his automatic reaction to their both getting into the same car. "When you've had more experience . . . " had been his introduction to thousands of remarks, and his invariable response to any mutual matter had always been what it was now: "I'll handle it."

What a fool I am, Christopher exploded inwardly. No wonder Dad left no message, no instructions, no advice, no duty, no *money* even, to me. He knew what a fool I am.

And from under his eyebrows, he looked at Ernie. "You want me to forget about it," he said.

Ernie looked a little surprised, but did not reply.

"Do you want me to forget Dad, too?"

Ernie contemplated him.

"Of course, you're a little jealous of me," Christopher went on. "You always have been. You always were a lousy older brother, I just thought I'd tell you that."

Ernie looked a little sadly at him. "All older brothers are lousy older brothers," he said.

"Why were you always so jealous of me? I'm not so great. Why did you always have to have *everything*? Why—"

"Shut up," cried Barbara, coming in from the vestibule, where she had been hesitating. "You can't say those things, Christopher, Ernie's sick. Do you have to say the worst things you can think of, now?"

Christopher didn't speak. But out of the side of his eye he saw and interpreted a little bit of mime: Barbara gesturing faintly toward the envelope and glancing toward Christopher ("Can't be allowed to read it?") and Ernie faintly but firmly shaking his head ("Never").

"I'm going now," said Christopher in a flat tone. "I hope you get better." And although Barbara moved to stop him, he left the room.

Out in front of the hospital was a square and he walked up and down for a while, up and down, and then finally took a taxi back to the center of Cairo. On the way it crossed the intersection where he had seen the body under the brown linen cloth. It had been removed and the group of conferring men was gone. No one had ever been interrupted more abruptly than that Egyptian, that man or woman who had been hit by a car, cut off in mid-breath, mid-thought.

The dead: through the pyramids and the solar boats and the very walls of the temples, they tried to speak. But, of course, they never succeeded in transmitting anything, here in Egypt or anywhere else.

Nothing ever came across, Christopher meditated, no communication was ever possible. To the survivor, no will was ever left, except his own.

He then felt very hungry. They were passing Shepheard's Hotel now and he asked the driver to let him off there. He went into the restaurant and ordered a steak. Malnutrition for an American with money in Egypt! he exclaimed to himself. Ernie. He really does need all the help he can get. And then he suddenly thought. Unlike me. I'll bet my father realized that. I'll bet he did. He realized I didn't need any posthumous letter of instructions or even any money; he had already given me and done for me and said to me what I needed; there's no other message coming. As a matter of fact, I don't need any message. It's too late for more instructions. There's just me, and that's enough. It has to be enough.

ABOUT THE AUTHOR

JOHN KNOWLES was born in Fairmont, West Virginia, and was educated at Phillips Exeter Academy and Yale University. He has been an associate editor for HOLIDAY magazine and a newspaper reporter.

His first novel, *A Separate Peace,* received the Faulkner Foundation Prize and the Rosenthal Award of the National Institute of Arts and Letters. Since its publication in 1969, *A Separate Peace* has become, along with *The Catcher In The Rye* and *Lord Of The Flies,* one of the most influential books in schools and colleges throughout the country.